T l. _ _ _ _ _ _R

OTHER BOOKS BY MICHAEL CISCO

THE TRAITOR

Michael Cisco

PRIME BOOKS

THE TRAITOR

———

Prime Books
www.prime-books.com

ISBN: 978-0-8095-7235-9

CHAPTER ONE

———

I rise from my pallet like a sleepwalker and cross the cell to the table, where I am writing this. I lay there all night in a trance, my eyes open, my body completely stiff, as if I were dead already and not dying; the effort to move is all but too much for me, in fact, it is too much for me, and I cause myself irreparable harm moving about. I am no doubt shortening my life at this moment as I write. When one blows on an ember it flares and thereby perishes all that much faster. I don't pretend to be "flaring," but something in me demands that I leave at least these few traces behind, as testimony, not to myself, but to why I came.

It's cold. There's no light, or very little light. Being who I am I may see in the dark. I have shriveled to a skeleton, not for being in here, but for the bug in my lung that I brought in with me. A few days ago, I have no idea how long it's been, I felt it spread to the other lung. I was lying on my pallet and I felt a sudden click in my chest as the bug punctured through to the other lung, and now it's in both. From that moment on I started coughing more and more until now I cough more than twice as much as I did before, and I am certain I will never leave this cell, that is, not entirely. It is because things have become so urgent in this way that I have turned to writing. Once things have become hopeless, it becomes possible to write.

I've just done some coughing. Each cough scatters against the walls and echoes back at me seeming even louder than when I coughed it. I have blood on my hand where I held it up to my mouth, and I can taste blood. My blood has never had what could be called *a strong flavor*. As I cough my lung's blood into my mouth and onto my hand, my coughs cascade through the room and are swallowed up, one by one, by the spirits. I'm sure they dote on each of my coughs, bearing as they do the increments of my death. When I die, when I am finished dying, when I've exhausted dying or dying has exhausted me, they will swallow me up in the same way, the same way they swallow my coughs, but also the same way I used to swallow them—the way I would swallow them all up now if I had the strength.

I will write down now who I am and some of my story, not so that you who read this, if there is anyone there, may understand me, since, in any case, you can't understand me; there is no way my story could make you understand me. I'm writing my story to prove that I understand it, and I can't help repeating it over and over to myself simply because that is all there is left of me. I favor it more for the useless details that remind me of how I used to be, not that I miss anything. Now I am nothing at all like I was, although I believe I am now what I had originally intended to be.

I write this first so I may arrive at my testament through these memories, as I arrived at where I am now through these times I'm remembering. If I don't write beautifully, it's because I'm trying to be honest, and because the taste of blood in my mouth reminds me how little time remains for me, how little time there is to polish words.

I must begin with my uncle my uncle Heckler, who had far more influence on me than my parents or brothers and sisters. My family was very large; I was lost in the middle. No one in my family liked my uncle Heckler, in fact, my mother and even my father, whose brother he was, detested him, but, since he was the only one of my relatives with any money, they had to put up with him. He looked nothing like my father, and was older. I remember he had a goblin's face, especially then, when every feature was absurdly elastic. He would grin, and it looked as if his mouth were going to stretch across the room. He grinned at everyone. He was also very near-sighted, and grinned at things as well. I realized he greeted everything he hated with that grin. There was also something womanish about his face, something that my father found especially disgusting. He looked exactly like his own father, while my uncle Heckler looked much more like their mother, who had abandoned the family. The last straw, or what would have been the last straw had my family not needed my uncle Heckler's money, was that my uncle Heckler had, at a young age—but not so young an age that he could have impulsiveness as his excuse—joined the apostates. This made him an object of hatred both for my family, and for the whole town, and placed him among a tiny religious minority within its walls. My uncle Heckler had to live apart in the town center, and I remember that, whenever he came to visit, he had to spend about twenty minutes outside our door, battering the dust from his shoes with his shapeless, loathsome old hat, before my mother would let him in.

My uncle Heckler took to me right away. He was always charming to my sisters, but even I could see that his heart wasn't in it. He grinned at them. My brothers didn't merit any attention as far as he was concerned. But I, for whatever reason, appealed to him, and my parents were glad to have someone to watch me. I was never large as a child, although I grew up bigger than the rest of them, and my brothers, even my younger brothers, liked to drub me. My uncle Heckler noticed me because I kept to myself, and because my parents didn't like me. My father beat me constantly, several times a week, but there was no getting used to it. He would stand in front of me, holding me by the collar of my shirt, and slap my face, first striking my left cheek with his open palm and then, reversing the direction of his hand, strike my right cheek with the back of his hand—as a result, my left cheek would sting more and more sharply while my right cheek would ache and throb, turning numb, and often my nose would bleed. Almost all my first teeth were knocked out of my head this way, when they loosened, they would fly out of my mouth as my father beat me. Occasionally I would lose my footing and tumble to the floor, and this would irritate him, and he would drag me to my feet with one hand and beat me all the more severely. I could always tell when he was about to beat me, because his face would go white, and his features would turn blank, and my mother would leave the room and lie down. I would stand there with my face uplifted, seeing only his implacable face, and soon I would lose all sense of my surroundings, until I was only my face, being struck with the regularity of a pendulum, at which point things to my view would become dark and colorless, until he released me.

When my uncle Heckler saw how much more frequently I was beaten than my brothers, he must have felt an affinity for me. He and I had both been, even from the very beginning, completely rejected by the world, and deprived of the world in every way. Having joined the apostates, my uncle Heckler was despised by the whole town, there wasn't a single person in the whole town who treated him honestly, he was swindled constantly, he was knocked aside in the street, he was harassed by young children, rocks and slops would come his way, and sometimes drunken men would shout at his house and the houses of the few other apostates in town. But the apostates enjoyed, if that is the word, official protection, and that set a strict limit on the amount of misery my so-called country men were able to impose on them. My uncle Heckler's affinity for me had been lost on me completely, until one day, by that time he must have seen what sort of person I was turning into, when his sudden arrival at the house saved me a thrashing. I recall he had come to talk to my father about money, and my father was positively seething with hatred for my uncle Heckler. I had wanted to leave altogether, for fear that my father would take this out on me, but my uncle Heckler, having concluded his business with my father, asked if he might take me out for a walk. My father, who was by that time completely overwhelmed with impatience, and, I'm sure, prepared to approve of anything that would rid him of my uncle Heckler more quickly, agreed. My uncle Heckler did not say anything much to me as we walked about, and we didn't walk more than a few dozen yards up the street. My uncle Heckler then stood and waited, and I, completely confused, waited with him. Eventually, my father left our house, as he did every evening, to play cards with his friends. Then my uncle Heckler brought me directly back to my door and sent me inside without a word. My uncle Heckler sent me back inside once my father was safely away. He would do this for me a number of times.

I was very fond of girls when I was a boy, and I chased them around the neighborhood, and they chased me. I was forever falling in love or fancying myself in love with one or another of them. This story is so disgusting I simply can't tell it quickly enough, nor could I tell it any worse. When I was a little older I fell in love with a girl who was a year or two ahead of me. She would have nothing to do with me. I already knew not to approach her—from that time on, I have never approached a woman myself. I thought about this girl every waking moment and it nearly killed me. I was starving myself, completely unable to eat, and I found it increasingly difficult to catch my breath. Then on one occasion I saw her with another boy of about her own age if not older still, and while he wasn't a brother of mine, he was precisely their type, indistinguishable from them, so that he might as well have been one of them, and of course the first moment they thought they were alone they turned to each other and began kissing. They had no idea anyone was watching. I stared at them. I recall this moment clearly; I was in excruciating pain, I felt myself dying, that is, I felt death, watching them; and as I watched and suffered with no clear sense of time, I felt also a desire or sense emerging out of this deadly feeling and, to put it badly, hovering over it, and I was seized by this feeling, this growing overpowering feeling, which seemed liable to overcome my pain, but which seemed just as liable to marry with the pain I was feeling, which grew forever, and amounted to a piercing longing to know how it felt to be him, how it felt to be her; I was drawn completely out of myself toward them by my desire to feel what they were feeling. How did that feel?—this demand hammered at me, and drove me right out of my mind, I would say; as I watched them I felt as if I were drilling my gaze into them and turning them to stone, but I also knew that they were alive, and I imagined I could palpably experience the life that was in them both, and the particular flavor of that life in that instant as the two of them met in those beastial kisses. How did that feel? How did that feel? After a while, it was only a nice little while for them, they left, and I remained where I was—I had been standing still watching them almost on the tips of my toes, taking a pounding of another type—I was disappearing, I thought, I let myself fall on my side, as if I were rather idly throwing my body into a corner, and, if I remember this right, I rolled onto my back, and I saw my uncle Heckler watching me intently from a few yards away. I read in the expression on his expressive face that he had seen everything, but moreover I knew that he had understood *perfectly* everything he had seen, and this was such a wild and foreign relief to me that I was able to close my eyes, and forgo making any effort. I allowed myself to be carried.

I was brought to my uncle My uncle Heckler's house, although I had never been there before. I am exhausted by this work, with a particular sort of exhaustion I felt for the first time as I lay under the window in My uncle Heckler's house. Lying there in a trance I watched him moving about in the room, looking for something. He didn't find it, and left the room. Apparently, he shortly thereafter sent word to my parents that I was ill and could not be moved for a few days, and that he would look after me until I "got better." To the present I have never "gotten better."

I stayed with My uncle Heckler then. We hardly spoke at all to each other during this time, and I believe I was all the better for it. I had never been in such a quiet house—although the neighborhood was anything but quiet. My parent's house was deafeningly loud by comparison with my uncle Heckler's house. I remember the walls were as bare as the walls of my cell, and the place was perhaps just as dingy—but it wasn't filthy, the way my parents' house had been filthy, and my parents' neighborhood had been filthy. My uncle Heckler had built all his own furniture; despite his incompetence with tools, he had insisted on it. So there was not a table or chair in the house that stood level on the ground, or did not seem at any moment about to collapse. Looking back, I can fully understand my uncle's preference for his own work, however badly-made, and his intolerance for any sort of ornamentation or decorating, and his work around the house seemed to me to be entirely typical of his way of doing things. He would inaugurate work on a piece of furniture, a table for instance, with a simple, but entirely practical and even ingenious, design in mind, and work on it with great care. But then he would run up against the inevitable snags, and, rapidly losing all patience, would bang the rest of the piece together all at once, in a kind of soured frustration to get the work over with. He was especially inept when it came to hinges, panels, and drawers—they were either so tightly fitted that they were impossible to open, or else they were only barely joined to the piece at all and prone to fall off. One corner of a table would be admirably worked with level wooden pegs, and then the others would be slapped together with nails, more nails at each corner, such that the last corner would be bristling with nails, most of them driven only halfway in and then bent down over the others and pounded down into the wood, creating an uncouth wen of bent nails.

I can't say I enjoyed staying with my uncle, but it was a relief. He didn't say a word about my fainting fit, and what went before, but I simply could not doubt, and do not doubt now, that he understood perfectly everything he had seen.

Three days after my fit, an old friend of my uncle's came to visit. He was a tall old man with bony wrists and a white beard, neatly trimmed, and he wore a great many complicated garments of shabby black material, not unlike what my uncle Heckler wore. They sat quietly together on a bench by the door and drank my uncle Heckler's wretched tea, talking in momentary fits and spurts, in low voices. I had never seen anything as dignified as the two of them, sitting together, alternately turning their heads to speak directly to each other's ears. The visitor looked at me a number of times, with none of the levity that so many old people affect when they have anything to do with young children, especially strange young children. He was looking frankly at me, and I started trying to think of some obliging way to justify his interest. At one point he came over to me and, without saying a word to me, took my hands and examined them closely, paying particular attention to the palms and fingernails. He also looked at my eyes and my forehead in an attentive, appraising way. I was not uncomfortable to be looked at like this. Shortly after, he said something briefly to my uncle Heckler that I did not catch, and left. That night, my uncle Heckler explained to me that his friend was an apostate, like himself, and we discussed this briefly. I expressed interest in the apostates, mainly, I believe, to please him. He nodded, as if to say this was certainly no surprise to him, and left me to sleep. The next morning I asked him again about the apostates, and we talked about this for a few hours, I asking him questions, he answering them. Finally he told me that his friend, and he, my uncle Heckler, were also both members of an apostate society, the Society of Blankness, being spirit-eaters, the two of them. The world being full of spirits, many of them dangerous or at least irritating and troublesome, he explained, the spirit-eater is the supernatural rat-catcher. He went on to say that the Society, which was the Society of the spirit-eaters, was comprised of persons whose souls were equipped, who knows why, with "blanks," who possibly may not have had souls at all, and who, by virtue of this empty or open spot, were able to consume and even to digest disembodied spirits. My uncle Heckler explained that the blank spot in the soul was the cavity into which the spirits could be drawn, much as the lungs draw breath. The visitor and he both were "blanks," as he put it, and they both had a strong suspicion that I was also blank. He explained to me that I was to become an apostate like himself, and that he and his friend would initiate me into the Society.

In a way it all seemed to be behind me already, or at least long-decided, long-assumed, and inevitable. And at the same time of course it was hopelessly unreal. What is a child of less than ten to understand in all this? I knew only that I would go where they asked me to go and do what they asked me to do, because they were the only people in the world who seemed prepared to bother with me at all.

My uncle's friend, whose name was Vyo, returned the next day with a cart, and together we went up into the foothills. The foothills there were naked, and one could at any point watch them recede into the distance all the way to the horizon in every direction, all identical, without much interference from trees or buildings. Vyo brought us to his village, which was an apostate village, situated on a rocky promontory jutting from the side of one of the higher of the foothills, or rather from one of the mountains at whose feet the foothills were gathered. The village was small and silent. We drove together in the cart along the muddy main street, and I could see many people, in fact every house was wide open and I could see practically every occupant—certainly every house was so wide open that only those residents taking refuge in the smallest rooms or crouched behind the low walls were out of view, and many of them, hiding from us, emerged prematurely as we passed and we saw them anyway. They all seemed a little frightened of one another, or withdrawn from each other; they clearly never spoke to each other except in desperate moments, and at that time I imagined they all seemed sad to me. The place was nameless and silent and sad to me, full of people who were essentially unable to speak to one another, because they were apostates. I also, already, felt unable to speak to any of them, and a little afraid of them, and after a time I felt unwilling to look at them any longer and gazed down into the cart.

Vyo brought me into his house, and there I was made an apostate and initiated into the Society. My apostasy was almost instantaneous—Vyo, in a weak, beautiful old voice, asked me a series of questions to which, as my uncle Heckler had previously instructed me, I did not respond. A brief and simple ritual, performed using only the most common household items readily to hand, converted me. As an apostate, as I remain now as I write, I felt no closer to them, no special fellowship, except in the sudden—I would call it an eruption if that weren't too sudden and explosive a word for what was a realization so slow in coming that I feel it has yet to fully arrive even now, forty or fifty years later—the feeling of being quietly sad was inserted into me (that's really no way to put it, but I don't want to dwell on it any more). I have, ever since, been gradually collapsing as a result, although I regret my apostasy no more than I regret being born—neither of them was avoidable. Nor was my meeting Wite avoidable, nor was my change as the result of meeting Wite.

My initiation into the Society of Blankness was also to a considerable extent my training, or at least the creation, within me, of the conditions that would make my training possible. The spirit-eater, they say, is guaranteed a livelihood, he will always have spirits to eat and so he will always have food to eat as well, that is actual physical food. This useful service which it was my privilege to join would in time indubitably present me with the opportunity to be of assistance to the most revered authorities.

There was little in the way of a regimen. Vyo began placing burning cold droplets in my eyes, more and more every day, and my eyes were always burning and smarting, especially when I rolled them in their sockets, when they would sting and the pain would increase so much I'd whimper and totter weakly against walls and furniture. I remember looking up at Vyo's long, pensive face as he would take my head in a single one of his big bony hands, and his soft fingers would rest lightly on my face, pulling my eyelids apart to apply the cold drops from the dropper. I had bad headaches and was constantly tired, but unable to sleep, and with little appetite. I couldn't think of anything but my painful eyes. Occasionally, and with no special enthusiasm, my uncle Heckler would assign me an exercise: I would be asked to look at a tiny tableau through a narrow hole, bored through a thick plank. I had to stare for very long periods of time through this miniature tunnel at a collection of dummies and doll furniture, or at small pictures, describing them in minute detail until my head began to swim and I could not keep my eyes in focus. I passed out at least once. My uncle later explained to me that this exercise had as its only point the production of these nauseated, faintheaded, painful states, and said that my last observations immediately before falling unconscious or otherwise failing were the only ones of any value.

Eventually, after some time, perhaps ten days, Vyo and my uncle Heckler set me in a chair, facing a mirror. The mirror was only a few inches away from my face, and they instructed me to do nothing but stare directly at my own image in the mirror until instructed to stop. The mirror was small, so that, as I sat before it, my face filled it, and the mirror in turn filled almost my entire field of vision. Vyo and my uncle watched me in silence. I am sure that at some point they simply left me alone, creeping stealthily out of the room. I sat and stared into the mirror, at my own face, without stopping. My eyes were in such pain that even moving them slightly was impossible—I had to stare straight ahead of me, into my own eyes, in the mirror. After only a few moments the outlines of my face were losing their distinctness, and I quickly lost any sense of recognition of my face. I stared motionless into the mirror, and in that time I seemed to be confronted with as many faces as there have ever been, all the possible faces stared back at me, including animal faces and the faces of buildings, trees, streets, rocks. I could not move, nor shut my eyes, nor even turn them away, and for no reason at all I stayed there and stared, feeling sickened, breathing very hard. Then all at once, suddenly, the mirror turned a blazing white, as if I were hanging only a few inches from the gleaming, polished surface of the moon, and the light was so bright it drowned out my reflection and shined right into my head, through my brains, so I could feel it at the back of my skull, on the inside. When I saw nothing but light, I knew, although at the time I had no way of knowing, or at least of saying or understanding this, that I was staring into the blank spot; what I did understand, precisely then, was that I had been staring at the mirror exactly as I had stared at the girl and her boy, when my uncle was watching, when he must have decided to bring me into the Society.

After that, I was worse than ever. I was awkward before, my father constantly reproached me for breaking things, everyone in town called me clumsy and called me stumbler especially. But from that time onward my entire body was a wooden limb, or I could also say, as Wite had said to me, that from that time on I was armored inside my body. Furthermore I could see that both Vyo and my uncle Heckler had the same clumsiness, and more—I could see the separate elements, the two sides of the automated statues that their bodies now were, and I knew without asking that they saw me in the same way. Not everyone appeared to me like this; for some, like my parents and siblings, and most of the people I have ever met, so I should say like most and not like some, there is a more or less complete harmony with the automaton so that it is more like a garment or a cosmetic, and less like a glass eye or false teeth, but this is also immediately clear to me on sight. My sight remained permanently altered, although what role the droplets played in this is unclear to me. I suspect they were simply intended to make use of my eyes painful.

One night, before I returned home, and I only mention this because I'm convinced I should, without any real reason and certainly without hope of being convincing myself, but one night, after being kept indoors for many days, I went outside. It seemed to me as though I were on the moon. I hadn't been allowed outside for days, and once I was out in the open air the hills were not familiar-looking, the world was unfamiliar-looking. The village was built of shavings from the moon, brilliantly white and blue, and it was so beautiful that I felt as if my heart was splitting, and tears poured out from around my cold, hard eyes. Disgusting as it might sound, I am not confessing this or saying it to be honest, but only to say it, that I was overwhelmed, and I seemed to be up among the cold forms of the stars, and I babbled to my sleeping uncle and to his friend Vyo in the house, thanking them over and over again because I was grateful to them for this. They kept mercilessly away from me, leaving me out among the stars, where I turned in every direction and, finding nothing, curled in on myself like a wood-shaving. I was frightened, by how beautifully every-thing struck me. The stars and the moon were perfectly silent and shining, and I could see the world remotely below me, possibly encased in a glass shell that would not readmit me, my having left. I was seeing spirits for the first time. My uncle explained this to me when he brought me in out of the street, where he had found me that morning, soaked with freezing dew, stiff and ill. I had nearly died, or so he claimed, in the street in the middle of the night, under the moon and an unusually clear sky, visible to the horizon on almost every side. It is insofar as I remain *there* that I am able to see spirits now, all around me as I write this.

Eventually my uncle brought me back to our town, down below, but not after many long, pointless days of sitting around Vyo's house in si-lence, looking out the windows, or down into the weak tea that Vyo would make for us. I believe now that my uncle was trying to save me the shock of returning home, or perhaps he saw that this was impossible, and was waiting instead for me to build up enough strength to survive the inevi-table shock. He told me nothing at all to prepare me, and so I was taken completely by surprise when we first arrived. As Vyo navigated the streets, steering us back to my uncle's house, I was assaulted on all sides by the spirits. This was the first time I experienced spirit as a massy weight pressing in from all sides as if they were trying to pop me right out of the world. I remember I had wanted to stare out at them all at first, and then I was so terrified the next instant that I buried my head in my uncle's coattails. I also remember him patting my head once or twice, because here as at every moment up to this point he had known exactly how I felt, and in hindsight I see how he must have reproached himself. He and Vyo both had long faces as they brought me into the house, and I don't doubt that they understood completely what they had done to me.

There were no spirits in my uncle Heckler's house, he had blanked them all. They wouldn't even come up to the windows, they were so afraid of him, and this was a relief for me, not having them around. I could watch them in safety, and then venture out among them, knowing I could run back inside if necessary. Now more than ever I stayed away from my old house and my family, and, with one exception, I didn't see any of them up close again for years. This exception being one of my older sisters, who came by my uncle Heckler's house to find out about me—she was the one who relayed to my parents the news that I had become an apostate and a spirit-eater. My parents were utterly disgusted with me and all but disowned me the moment they found out, as if this were necessary considering they had never actually owned me in practice. That final rejection was something we had both seen coming for years, for almost my entire life up to that point, and whether we understood it or not, that was what we were both waiting for. At that point, my parents were more or less free of me, and I was more or less free of them. When it happened, I felt, for the first time, as if I missed them—but I did not return to see them. Now I think that I did not miss them at all—what I was missing was what I ought to be missing. Formally, I missed them, but not really. Certainly, not those people.

In the year or so that followed, my uncle Heckler taught me to read and write, although my stupidity so exasperated him that he gave up several times, and had to be persuaded by Vyo to take up with me again. Some of his other apostate friends would drop by every week to teach me math and history, with limited success. Then afterwards they would sit together by the door in the summer and by the fireplace in the winter, eating peanuts soaked in coffee. I learned from them about the Alaks, who had brought the apostasy when they invaded, a very long time ago, at least four generations. They had sewn our country into their patchwork Empire and had installed a governor to rule us. Many of my uncle Heckler's friends, including Vyo, had ancestors who had collaborated with the Alaks, and converted to their religion as well, perhaps to curry favor. The Alaks interfered very little with the interior workings of the country. The people still lived much as they always had. They all hated the Alaks, to such an extent that the rulers and their retinue had to jail themselves in their garrisons, emerging only under heavy guard, and keeping always "underground." There was an Alak garrison in my town, and had been since before I was born, but I had caught only a few brief glimpses of the Alaks themselves. I understood that there were more in the capital. At the time I was curious about the Alaks, but no one in my family had wanted to talk about them. The apostates seemed to be on good terms with them—I was surprised to learn that many of them were meeting with the Alaks regularly, mostly for religious services, and there was perhaps some sort of pensioning or dispensation for the descendants of the collaborators as well. At the time, they told me only that the message of the Alaks was *love*, and that they ruled not because they were the best of all people, but were the best of all people because they had been selected to rule, I presume by Providence, and that this might change at any time, so the Alaks believed. They did not, and still do not, insist that this selection had anything to do with them personally. They were eager to assure the world that they did not consider themselves superior, they were eager to be accepted by the people they conquered.

It was at one such religious meeting that it was decided I should go to the capital of the province with another one of my uncle Heckler's friends, a woman whose name I've forgotten. I did. I spent my adolescence there, in the capital, and became what is called a success. And when, on one occasion, I found the time to return home to visit my uncle Heckler I learned that he had died. His body had been stolen before it could be buried and was presumably burnt or discarded on the outskirts of town by partisans. I saw one of my sisters in the street that day, and she didn't recognize me. I didn't make myself known to her. She saw how I was dressed (as an apostate, in an Alak garment) and she spat, but she saw only an apostate, not her brother, who would have inspired in her an even deeper loathing. The few apostates remaining who had known me as a child told me everything, feeding me peanuts soaked in coffee, about how Vyo had been torn under a runaway cart and languished for three months before he died. The only spirit eater in the vicinity, who could have helped him, was deliberately sent away. Who there in town would have carried a letter to me in the capital? Not a single letter reached me. I never stopped crying the time I was there.

CHAPTER TWO

———

I returned to the capital and forgot about my home town, never mind what it was called. Let that name be forgotten. If I hadn't made a deliberate effort to forget about home, to insist that the capital was my only home, I would have been completely unable to work. My home town was never anything really like a home to me in the first place; I thought of it as my "home" only because I'd never had anything more like a home; it was a habit of mind, and nothing more. The longer I stayed away, the more wrong it seemed to call it home, as the mere, the meagre web of associations that bound me to it, that were all that made it anything like my home, disappeared, until finally I was offended and ashamed to call it my home town—but what else could I call it? The capital was no home to me either, although I had perhaps less cause to feel that way. What do I mean? The capital was no home to anyone. There were more apostates, I hesitate to say "like me" because they were not converts and they were nothing "like me"—they were born apostates, and so they were nonetheless strangers to me. They did practically nothing together, not as apostates; even their, our, infrequent rituals were sparsely attended, and often the native celebrants were outnumbered by the representatives of the Alaks, who were very polite and full of respect, but who refused to have anything to do with any of us.

I distinguished myself as a spirit eater—I "made a name" for myself. I have no idea what was said about me, or how such notions take form in general, but, after a few years, the Alak representatives hired me to spy for them. Everyone in the capital employed spirit eaters, the city was seething with spirits, they would have utterly ruined the town if it weren't for the spirit eaters. A town filled with spirits is oppressive, the memory of such towns is too good, no one can forget, nothing goes away, death hovers everywhere, fragmentary remains of grasping lives poison the air, and as soon as a space is cleared it is newly infested. Many of my clients went on to become my "victims," there was no end of call for me, and I could get in anywhere. It was impossible to work with people the way I did and not absorb an infinite number of incidental data, and these were for some reason invaluable to the Alak representatives. Let me be clear—I never worked with the Alaks themselves, only their local deputies and imported officials. Actual Alaks were pointed out to me only very rarely and at a distance. I impassively answered all the questions that were put to me by the authorities and met every request that was made of me. I went from house to house like a machine, without the slightest concern, utterly neutral. When arrests followed, I stood by the road and watched the armed men, watched the suspects being brought, bound, out to the street and carted away, all with a statue's face. There is nothing to be said about those days—they were a blank. Blanking was my business. I blanked everything to my level; I leveled and cleared away the rubbish, and it was all rubbish then. Now there is Wite, who is with me at this moment as I write, *at this very moment,* and every moment, as I lie awake, as I glance up at the window and the moon in its branches, and he is clearing *me* aside, if I haven't been cleared already, if I wasn't born clear and off to one side in the first place. Wite also guarantees me, that I am still here, still the one I've always been, because he never allows me any solitude. I am completely alone, but I'm alone with Wite, and so I can't disappear. I can't disappear until I disappear into Wite, or until he lets me disappear. I am sustained by Wite, who also compels me to subsist against my will, such as it is. I'm exhausted. Now Wite pulls my strings, and I have only enough strength left over to succumb. There is so little to be said about me. As I write, that little is reduced more and more.

I married. My wife died fifteen years later of the disease that is killing me now—that will kill me. We can't do anything about this disease. A rag that has been thoroughly soaked in water can absorb no more, no matter how long one holds it in the stream, and under the effects of this disease a spirit eater is like that rag, he, or she, can take nothing in, not even to be healed.

We had one child, a son, who has by now utterly disowned me. He moved back to my home town and attached himself to my parents and brothers and sisters, and, by bringing things as it were full circle, has precisely and deliberately erased me as if I had never existed for him. Disgusted by my so-called crimes, he has evicted me from his life, or rather this is what he believes he is doing—if anything he has bound himself more tightly to me by making it his life's work to get free of me than he would ever have been as merely my son. Now I have mentioned them both, my family, and now I will pass on to other things and mention them no more, except to say that they deserved better.

What is it like to step into the midst of people and to be immediately accepted, to have a place made for you and to step into it immediately, at the first possible instant, falling into step with the others, perfectly naturally? How does it feel to meet and embrace someone—does your heart shine like the sun? I am unable to speak convincingly about such things because I've never felt anything of the kind; I've never even felt as if I ought to feel that way, but for some reason could not, at any time. The people surrounding me, with whom I'm supposed to have so much in common, and with whom I actually have nothing in common—these people make no impression on me of any kind. No matter how I deal with them, or under what circumstances we meet, they might as well not be there, they might as well be anyone else, or perhaps it would be better to say that I might as well be anyone else, or be not there at all, for the difference it would make. None of my so-called compatriots could touch me in any way. If what they say is true, and they shine with compassion and fellow-feeling when they meet each other, then I am on the other side, with Wite. Wite and I were alone together, and for that reason we had everything in common. Wite has taken complete possession of me. Almost complete possession of me. Wite is the person I should be. I can never be Wite, and so there is nothing left for me but to testify for him here. There is a white patch on the door, and in the dark I can see it almost shining, and it looks to me like Wite's face, and I imagine his face sliding into view through the door, his eyes shut, his face blank, as it was when he died. Likewise I have stopped up the window with my old satin housecoat, feeling the cold so little now, and the moonlight that is reflected from the smooth stone of the windowsill shines up on my robe, lighting the creases from below, and together they resemble Wite's face. The spirits circulate through the room from the patch on the door to the satin robe, impaled on the irregular edges of the bars at the top of the window, and then back to the patch again, like current between the two poles of a battery, and this is an entirely appropriate image, which is why I include it. They rush back and forth with the greatest possible speed, as if it were urgently necessary to get across the room, and then they turn back again as if they were momentarily confused, as if they were hunting something down, they seem to miss me time and again.

I stopped up the window because it distracts me. Even in the middle of the night there's no end of scurrying on the street below. The capital was like that; people wasting their time running crazily from place to place, getting more and more frantic until they're prepared to shove people out into the traffic, trample them underfoot, so desperate are they to get to whatever trivia they have to do, and this can only produce more of the same hysteria. A round of ordinary business, buying a few articles here and there, is an exhausting task, and you stagger back through your door four hours later as if you'd just been in a fistfight. People point to the so-called intellectual life in the cities, especially in the capitals, but how could it be otherwise, even the purest simpleton is bound to start asking "why" when he's confronted with these heaps of disgusting people everywhere. When there is always someone to occupy the space you have only just vacated, where every breath you draw and every morsel of food you take is pulled right out of someone else's mouth, how can you help but ask by what right you take them, and especially, by what right do the others demand them of you? No one who lives in a city can manage it except at the expense of devouring others, even if a single killing is spread out over several victims. Even the simplest task becomes as draining as a fistfight when the city is involved. Every task, no matter how inconsequential, becomes absurdly overwrought in the city, where you have to struggle like a prize-fighter merely to keep your head above water. By comparison, my rise, such as it was, was effortless. There are few spirit-eaters to begin with, despite the demand, few that actually practice, few who are actually able to do it well enough, or who do it consistently, or who care to do it for a living. Certainly a great many would be offended at the prospect of becoming a spirit-eater, that is to do it professionally. Many of "my circle," certainly most of the Alak representatives, regarded me as a kind of prostitute. I was more or less a successful prostitutor of my "little gap of soul."

I became a spy for the Alaks and improved my standing immeasurably.

They took me on and gave me a salary, and saw to it that I had nothing but rich and influential clients, the kind with secrets they wanted to know. These were not secrets for me, because blanking demands that everything be made open and drawn out, out, if not into the light, at least out. I would enter a home and, when it was made still, I would allow the gap in me to draw the spirits out, like a tiny whirlpool that empty spot in me would draw them out and through it into me, where they would become that empty spot, blank. And as I "ate" them, they would have to give up everything, all their power, all their strength and will, their intelligence such as it was, their memories, and all these would be surrendered to me. I, at no cost to myself, could then give over to the Alak representatives those things that they wanted. The work was simple. I was like a statue, no like an implement, in so many different hands. I did nothing for myself, or as little as possible.

The details of this life are not important, not relevant, not even interesting. I only insisted that I keep going, and to do this I had to keep my head down low, and keep my eyes on the ground, and do nothing to waste my flagging energy, but to stare fixedly at that distant point where perhaps things would begin to open for me once again, or where things would finally close to me altogether, this difference was something I didn't make much of. Wite also had this stare—it was one of the first things I had noticed about him. From his pupils came two fine grey threads of almost invisible light, thin as hairs, perfectly straight, stretching out before him like railroad tracks; when the tracks are laid, the train must then travel down those tracks and remain on them at every moment, or jump the tracks and be crushed by its own force. His gaze, like mine, cut everything away but that narrow beam on which he advanced. Those two threads stretched into his eyes and down into a gap inside like mine, or, since a gap is just nothing, with no substance of its own, it would be more correct to say that those two threads fell from the gap, upon which he and I both opened. The gap is a void that folds in on itself and is infinite, forever escalating its demands. This is what eats the spirits, although to speak of eating in this case is misleading—the spirits are eaten in the same way that a diver is eaten by the water; I mean that no active relation may be attributed to the water. I think that the action is the spirits', and not any property of the whirlpool. I think they draw themselves to it.

When I have eaten a spirit, I do not feel filled up with it, in fact I don't feel it at all, but I discover its vitality in myself accidentally. This vitality simply appears somehow in me, without my noticing. People used to remark on how well-preserved I once looked. Were I not so ill now, I would look younger than I am. When I finished blanking to the client's satisfaction, I was then bound by the rules of the Society, which had an entirely different character in the capital than in my home town or in Vyo's town, which was almost a secret army in the capital, I was bound by its strictest rule to then dispense what surplus of vital animation I had accumulated in my work in the service of a number of charities organized by the Society. In particular, there were wards and wards of sick children, many dying, who were languishing for want of money to pay the doctors. Once or twice a week I would pass down a different aisle of beds, pressing my hands on their foreheads, transferring the animation I had stored to them, as ordered. After a few months of this I felt I knew more about disease than any doctor, because of course I had touched it time and again, in the wards, touched it directly, and I had felt it recoil and shrink when I touched it. And now, of course, I know disease the way one would know an old wife, but now I am too weak and too accustomed to try to drive it away. That doesn't mean it doesn't frighten me. It does frighten me.

Wite was a spirit-eater, like me, for a while. When I met him, he had become what they, the Society, call a "soul-burner"—he had started hoarding the spirit-power, and was "burning" it to sustain himself, or to overreach himself, to overcome his human limitations. How childish that sounds! He simply began using it as he wished, and paid no attention to the Society, he seemed to forget the Society altogether and all at once. As a consequence of this so-called "misuse," the soul-burner becomes more and more spirit-like; his body begins to deteriorate. When a member of the Society is labeled a "soul-burner," he is immediately considered to be under censure, and a warrant is put out for him. You see how different the Society is in the capital! If he doesn't take steps to undo what he has done, then after a very brief time he is labeled an "incorrigible" and thereafter he is subject to summary execution. In practice, a soul-burner is considered incorrigible from the start; in practice he receives no grace period. I was preparing to retire, and had never encountered a single soul-burner, when news of Wite reached me. I was told he was a foreigner who had been living in the western part of the country for a few years, still young, and under suspicion from the start. When it became clear that steps to censure him were underway, he disappeared, apparently heading for his home, in Heipacth. His journey would bring him into the vicinity of the capital. I was told he was in the woods, making his way to the border on foot. He was described to me by the Alak representatives as something of an ogre, pillaging isolated homes, leaving behind him a trail of victims, racing with inhuman speed through the forest with gore dropping from his hands, this a typical Alak description, the Alaks were the greatest war-mongers in the world but the prospect of violence always filled them with a kind of abstract dread just the same, they wrung their hands over isolated and strange violence just the same. My so-called "fellow-countrymen" were anxious and frightened. Our Prince Eskellde, who now took his orders from the Alak governor, took steps to secure the city and assembled a party to find Wite. They made their preparations with the greatest possible publicity, but the Prince seemed genuinely determined to be satisfied only by Wite's death, that they should not return without his carcass. At the last minute it was decided that I should accompany them, despite my age, as a gesture from the Alak representatives. I protested, but my so-called superiors would not even speak to me or admit me into their presence—I was informed by letter that I was to go. Even so, I draughted a refusal and submitted it to them. I was informed that my letter had reached the Alak representatives in lamentable condition, but that I should not be concerned, and that it was taken for granted that I really had every intention of going, that I naturally understood I would be arrested if I did not. That I understood my so-called expertise in this area, as the leading spirit-eater in the capital, in actuality the leading Alak spy in the capital, would be indispensable to the party.

I attended the hunting party. I was given a horse that I was unable to ride. The sheriff, whose name was Yestyy, came up to me and handed me a pistol, telling me to "Shoot Wite at first glance." Wite was described to me, very badly as I know now, and a number of different gestures and spoken signals were discussed. Yestyy assigned himself to me as my partner, and in pairs we entered the forest, following a number of chasers on foot with their bloodhounds, and led between the trees by the Prince.

Whenever I picture Wite to myself, I picture him running in the cold

MICHAEL CISCO

humid air between the trees. We caught sight of him time and again, always in front of us, sometimes off to one side and then almost immediately
he would be off to the other side. I could make him out only as an obscure
patch moving in and out of view in the distance. There was no place he did
not seem to be. He appeared and disappeared. I saw him only intermittently, but despite this, I could see very clearly that he was somehow on
fire. He was enveloped in fire. A transparent flame played about his body
from head to foot, and his body seemed to emit, even in complete silence,
as I discovered later, a thunderous, inaudible roar that made the air shud-
der rigidly as he passed through it. At one point, he appeared close by. He
jumped from a high bank overhanging a dry riverbed, and landed on his
feet with a deafening report, and the sand around his feet flew back in all
directions. Wite merely straightened himself and vanished into the trees
again. The men pursued him, and I followed. They were frightened, and
eager, and carried rifles which they held low to the ground. We were all
going faster every moment. At this point we had fanned out in a long line
several riders deep. The dogs, and the birds in the trees, together with the
hooves of the horses and the random shot, were all I could hear—except
that at times I would hear Wite scream from far ahead, this from the great
effort he was making. Wite's screams were brittle and metallic, and they
hung motionless in the air, they hung motionless in the air like hanged
men. I was terrified, but unable to control my horse, and it followed the
others. We were so deep in the woods that on all sides there were nothing but trees, very old, very black, and their boughs closed out the sun,
whose light was grey. I only wanted to escape. Wite was all around us, he
seemed to flash in and out among the horses, and I saw his pale ghostly
face, glaring, furious, flashing past ahead of me in the shadows of the
trees. Wind flooded over me and I saw it brought with it the flavor of
something invisible that was coming, and then I heard men and horses
screaming ahead of me, and dogs howling, my horse jerked back as if he'd
been shot and I was nearly knocked from my saddle, leaving me hanging from its side, and I jumped down. My horse staggered back past me.
I was terrified and I went to hide myself behind a tree. Riderless horses
fled by me, the whites of their eyes showing on all sides and their mouths
stretched open and frothing, and the dogs raced between the horses. The
screams had already stopped, but for just a moment I had heard a sound

26

of pounding and thumping, and the ground had shook beneath my feet. I buried my head in my hands and heard nothing but shrieking birds and more screaming from all sides.

I found myself at the edge of a small clearing, hiding by a tree. A number of the men who had ridden out ahead of me were lying dead on all sides. They had been smashed to pieces against boulders and trees. Yestyy was there, mortally wounded. He had been crushed; he was covered with blood. I looked up, and Wite was standing in the clearing, his profile turned to me, glaring now at Prince Eskellde, who was standing, unhurt, a dozen paces from him. The Prince was petrified. I watched Wite raise his hands, and I saw the flame burst out all over him. The Prince was seized up, all his muscles went rigid, and his eyes were growing wide. As I watched, his face became unrecognizable, and disappeared, it became nothing but features. Wite's face was also disappearing, becoming strange and transfigured, as if he was receiving a revelation. Yestyy called to me as he died, in a voice thick with blood, pointing weakly at the pistol I held in my hand. "Shoot him! He is distracted!"

"Shoot him!"

I did not shoot.

CHAPTER THREE

I was the only survivor. I survived because I had put the pistol in my coat pocket and fetched my horse for Wite. I had watched him tear Prince Eskellde's soul from his body, and snuff it out like spitting on a spark. He then devoured the Prince's dead soul, which he had killed. It was only after he had finished devouring the Prince's dead soul that his face resembled itself again. His face shone with sublime ruthlessness; he was wan and exhausted from the chase, but his obvious frailty only made the strength his will shine more forcefully. Looking at him, I was afraid he would suddenly fly apart under the pressure of his own will. The prospect of Wite flying apart terrified me; it's the most terrifying thing in the world to watch someone disintegrate in front of you. Someone collapses in the street, an epileptic, and right before your eyes you see his face dissolve, and you are suddenly looking at someone who isn't anyone in particular, who is suddenly no more human than a statue or a cadaver. No one who hasn't seen such a thing with their own eyes can imagine what a shock it is, how a shock like that can ruin you. Only a moment before I had seen the Prince's face ebb out of sight, and become inhuman, as Wite drew his soul out. In the same moment I had seen Wite's face convulse and become inhuman. But I had not been paralyzed, Yestyy had distracted me with his words. I chose not to shoot.

I put the gun away, and I turned to fetch my horse for Wite. I was not afraid that he would kill me, not afraid to turn my back on him to get my horse, which was standing nearby, watching us both. I led it into the clearing, and it followed passively. I remember thinking what a good horse it was, and that we felt alike then as we re-entered the clearing. Wite watched me approach, and I asked him if he wanted my horse. He had not moved. He stood still in the clearing, and the body of Prince Eskellde was lying in front of him. Suddenly, he said, "No, I want the Prince's horse," and went off to find it. He called over his shoulder, "you can keep yours."

I saw him mount the Prince's horse. Prince Eskellde's horse allowed him to mount, and turned with him toward the foothills. I mounted my own horse and followed him—he rode awkwardly and it was not difficult to catch up and ride with him.

What a lot of nonsense I'm writing! You can't understand why I didn't shoot! I wrote that I chose not to shoot—a stupid, irresponsible thing to say! I watched him turn to Prince Eskellde and rip his soul out, extinguish it, and devour it. He was demonic—don't look to me for explanations, I can only say that he was demonic, he was filled with demonic ruthlessness, and I could not shoot him. Even exhausted, as he was, he was demonic, he was supernaturally strong and overflowing with this strength—it was a miracle, and no one who has never seen a miracle can understand what it means to see one. It means that something impossible has happened. Anyone could say that a miracle is something impossible, but they say it thoughtlessly, mindlessly, because most people have such weak imaginations they couldn't possibly understand what they're saying when they say that a miracle is something impossible. Ask anyone what that means, what it means to see a miracle, and they will say that it's something impossible, but they mean that a miracle is something formerly believed to be impossible that turns out not to be, not to be impossible, in other words, but possible after all. If this were really true, then miracles would be the most ordinary things in the world, the most uninspiring things in the world, and what can one expect from people who have never been anything but ordinary and uninspired.

I have seen a miracle—I saw something that was impossible. This happened and I saw it with my own eyes—I saw Wite there in the clearing, standing in a sheet of flame, and I saw him devour the Prince's soul with strength showering out of him, and this wasn't what was impossible, I knew such things were possible, though I had never thought for an instant that I would ever witness such things. Wite was impossible. Wite was a miracle. I did not shoot him then because I worshipped him then. From the start, I was somehow in awe of him, to think what he had done, but when I saw him with my own eyes, in the clearing, I worshipped him. I put away my gun and offered him my horse, and it was entirely natural. Inconceivable that I should then turn my back to him and fetch him my horse, that I should hear him speak normally to me, and that I should ride along with him as he fled toward his own country; inconceivable that he should have a country, that he could speak normally with anyone after what he had done, that anyone who had been a child, who had had parents and a home town, that anyone human could have done what he did, and not simply that, not simply doing it, but being what he was. Now do you understand, do you have any idea at all? How could you?

He did everything I described, he was everything I have said he was, and he was like a divine being. I rode alongside him and talked with him, ate with him, when he ate, slept near him, when he slept, I held his head when he had to vomit, as he often did, and at the same time I worshipped him. So, for the duration of our time together, I was impossible. How could I speak to him normally, after seeing what he was? I can't think how. I can't understand myself with him any more than I could understand him. It would be more correct to say that I have always been impossible, and the same was true for Wite, but for him that meant strength, because he was selfish—he was inconceivably, impossibly selfish; there is nothing anyone could compare his selfishness to, there is no conceiving this selfishness in ordinary terms; but for me it meant impotence, because I was not selfish, not in any way, because I practically had no self at all.

I remember, Wite and I rode the rest of the day together and well into the night, well after dark. He seemed to have no need for light, and he urged his horse on through the forest, which was of course absolutely black—nothing at all was visible. We were passing through rough, invisible terrain, blind, seeing only the few objects nearest us as patches of denser darkness against the darkness. We stopped when Wite fell from his saddle. At first I did not realize he had fallen—I was nearly collapsing myself, nodding and tilting nearly from the saddle, jerking myself awake again only to peer in confusion at the featureless blackness ahead. I knew Wite was near, because I could hear his horse battering through the bracken. The bracken rose up as high as my stirrups, we had unthinkingly ploughed into it. I was so tired I leaned forward and pressed my face against the stinking mane of my horse, I had to put all my trust in my horse and gave up directing it. A moment later I was awake again, feeling alert but unable to think, and it took me a few moments to understand that my horse's head was bobbing, it was nuzzling Wite's horse. I spoke without thinking, and Wite's voice came from below and to the right. He said, "I've fallen." From the tone of his voice I knew that he was exhausted and unwilling to move again. I dismounted and fell unconscious. All of our days ended like this, all of our days took shape along the same simple plan of flight until collapse. Wite was like a train, he could only go on and on, and when he spoke he had the same quality of bearing down on me, his voice would fall on my ears barring all other sounds. And in his manner, there was the same shocking shrill mineral quality of a train whistle, when he would stop and turn his profile to me in the cold humid air between the trees.

He was entirely blue and white, like the upper atmosphere where the air is thinnest and the clouds are frozen. He was as clean as the upper atmosphere, and his body and clothes smelled like ice. When we needed food I would be dispatched to the nearest city. These cities were all alike, with clean hands and faces and filthy under their clothes. Even as a so-called citizen of the capital I had slunk down the street with my head between my shoulders, and through these tiny cities I passed, beneath notice. I would bring the food back to Wite, and he, revolted at the sight of it, would insist that we ride as fast as we could manage for several hours, at least half the day, before he would consent to stop and eat. Waiting for me to return, he would get anxious; he would literally nearly lose his mind in his anxiousness to go, and he would look at me with hate, for keeping him waiting, when I came back. The strain of waiting offended his impatience, and that he should then have to wait for food, which repulsed him, was unbearable. But he also needed to exhaust himself to the point of being nearly incapacitated with pain before he would consent to eat. When Wite ate, he would cram as much food as possible into himself without chewing, or with as little chewing as he could physically manage. Wite needed practically no food at all; he was already at the point when a soul-burner becomes more dependent on spirits than on food. Wite ate in a fury, and he was ashamed that he still had to eat. I believe he could have survived on even less food than he ate, but he vomited so much of it back up again that he was forced to eat more than was necessary. He always waited until the decision to eat was taken out of his hands, until he had either to eat or collapse entirely, permanently. He hated his own entrails, and gave them as little satisfaction as he could—all spirit-eaters have something like this feeling, imagining the nerves and all the clean parts of the body pulling away in revulsion from the entrails, imagining a solid body with no separate internal parts, of wholly the same substance, and this is what I discovered when I was a boy, when my body suddenly seemed to me to be only a sort of wooden leg. Wite would say that he was armored in his own body. He expressed himself in childish ways. He would tell me that eating was an addiction, and this word "addiction" was especially hateful for him. Anything that compelled him was hateful to him. Wite said that he hated smokers, he had particularly bitter hate for smokers, for anyone who cultivated special needs and smokers above all. He called smoking the most disgusting habit of a civilization that is nothing but disgusting habits. Eventually his disgust became so acute that he, as he said, would retch every time he smelled smoke.

This was how he became a soul-burner: he loathed smoking. The smell of smoke indoors is hateful but it's possible to escape it by going out of doors, but when one is out of doors in the so-called fresh air the smell of smoke is intolerable, and one day when a man walked by in front of him on the street and a cloud of smoke came in his direction Wite reached out in a very simple way and snatched the man's soul from his body like a long plume of smoke, extinguishing and devouring it like he extinguished and devoured the soul of Prince Eskellde. I had never heard such a beautiful story. I was fascinated at the new idea of selfishness. I cannot say this without failing miserably, I can only say over and over again that I worshipped him because he was willing to go to the furthest possible extreme over a trifle. He was absolutely intolerant of anything, no matter how small, that offended him, and he was entirely willing to risk his life like that, to avenge the very least of infractions.

As a spy for the Alaks I conducted a thousand experiments on the people around me, and without exception I was unable to deny the childishness of these people. In every case, the parents are simply craftier versions of the children, but with the same childishness. I could not deny that I was the same. As I would walk down the street, and I seem to remember doing nothing else, I felt precisely the same as I had once felt looking up at my father as he struck me back and forth across my face. The colossal buildings that loomed on all sides had the same expression as my father's face had had, set to crush the life out of me with nothing but brutality and indifference. I knew other people who felt this way, and who slipped out from under by becoming reckless, or ridiculous. Wite got out from under through simple, thorough, selfishness. It takes a light touch to be that selfish. I had never had a light touch, I had never had the courage to be reckless, so I was left to struggle, using every ounce of my desperation, just to keep my head above water. At every moment I was in danger of being swept underneath the ice, crushed under a glacier—I'm overdoing it, but there was forever this sense of catastrophe hanging over me, I mean the risk of strangling on my own resentment. Now I lie in this cell and feel the weight of my tombstone crushing my chest, with resignation and fear, but with no giving up. I had walked the streets of the capital as if I had my coffin around my shoulders already and I felt it bearing me down to the ground, gradually wearing me away. When I met Wite, he and I fled together through the trees like errant cadavers.

Once we nearly blundered into a small village, farther up in the mountains. We had to reverse ourselves for a mile or so and take a higher, more tiring route through the trees. After a time we descended past the outskirts of the town, I never learned the name. By this point Wite and I were both of us completely exhausted. Below us, in a depression between two bulges of rock, there was a cemetery. By instinct Wite and I immediately took refuge there. Cemeteries are always the only refuge. The slope was steep and the grass was slick with dew, so that we were at great pains to make our way down to shelter behind the row of mausoleums. Covered with clumps of earth and grass, I had been the first to make it to the level path between the mausoleums, and Wite was coming along behind me, moving slowly and in great pain because he was starving. I looked up and saw a gravedigger

standing below us, and both Wite and I stopped. The gravedigger had noticed us at once, and was staring up at us with a shocked look on his face. I felt as if I had an instant rapport with this gravedigger, as I have always felt with every gravedigger I've met. This was the first of a long series of identical gravediggers who gave us shelter as we traveled to Wite's country. Gravediggers and spirit-eaters do complementary work, we dispose of human refuse, the most human sort of refuse, and the most intolerable sort of refuse. Cadavers and spirits are human refuse, and they are absurdly difficult to dispose of properly. When someone dies, a small gang of specialists is required to remove and inter the body in such a way that it can always be located precisely at any time while preventing it from ever appearing again. Wite horrified people because he was dead but they could see him, and because he wandered, was everywhere at once, even when he was with me. A spirit-eater must make himself into a graveyard for spirits. Wite, as a soul burner, had obviously become a graveyard for spirits. He had become a mausoleum for spirits. He had become his own grave. The gravedigger is also the one who keeps the graves, and it is expected of him that he will see to it that the graves remain closed and the dead are kept down. This gravedigger recognized Wite and me at once, and we recognized him. I believe that he knew who we were. Now he led us to one side, to the mortuary chapel. He entered through the side door and deliberately caused the door to swing wide open behind him with an outstretched hand, allowing Wite and me to follow him inside. Like all gravediggers, his body was ponderous, and he smelt of the soil. He had large hands, and, when he turned to us in the chapel, his face had an unusual, cagey look. Like all gravediggers he was a grave himself, filled with the dangerous and unwholesome secrets of the people he buried, clearly preferring the helpless and embarrassing cadavers the townspeople hastily delivered into his hands with disgust to the people themselves. He offered us the hospitality of the mortuary chapel and brought us water. I watched him through the windows lumbering back and forth between the chapel and the shed where he lived. He moved awkwardly when he moved fast. I later saw him digging another grave on a hummock above the chapel—before this, I had never been in a cemetery where it was possible to walk below the level of the graves. It was twilight. The gravedigger seemed to be working in a blue haze. The sun was shining up on the clouds from below the horizon. Our arrival had refreshed him, because he dug into the ground remarkably fast, first rolling back the sod and breaking up the clay with a pick, then ripping up enormous clods of earth. The pile of earth beside him grew quickly. He struck the ground with such force that I could feel the reverberations in the wall of the chapel. I then watched him bring the tombstone, carrying it over his head, although it was as heavy as he was.

A body was laid out in the center of the chapel. The upper portion of the coffin lid was hanging open on its hinges. A young woman was inside, her hands bound on her chest by a loose bandage around her wrists, her head swathed in gauze so that only her blue face was visible. She had been dead for at least a week. Wite pointed out that she had been pregnant. He and I lay on opposite sides of the chapel with the bier between us. The gravedigger had brought in a few bags of compost for us to lie on. Before he went to rest, Wite had stood over the body and stared at its face, staring at it, I want to say "mechanically" although I know this conveys nothing. The night passed.

I had thought this was a nightmare: I could hear the dead woman wailing, this went on for hours, I would notice it again and again, realize to my shock that this was the same wailing I had heard earlier, that she was still wailing, it seemed she was sobbing for hours, for her own destruction. She stopped abruptly, I thought at the eruption of Wite's voice. I heard her speak without understanding, but from the tone of her voice I thought she was bargaining. Wite's voice was brutal and flat when he said, "yes." After a pause the wailing began again, and continued until I awoke in the morning. I was disoriented and unsure as to whether I had woken up because the wailing had not stopped. The woman's body was contorted, and her face had the blank, unrecognizable, ruined look of someone whose soul has been devoured—oily tears had carved streaks in the dust on her face. A naked, squalling baby lay on her now-flat stomach, angrily snatching at the air with its fingers.

Wite was standing by the door, he had been dozing on his feet, leaning against the jamb, and I saw that his right hand was covered in filth. With this hand he opened the door of the mortuary chapel and stepped outside, moving with renewed energy. Later on he explained to me that the purpose of spirit-eaters was to clear away old rubbish. He said that spirit-eaters turned their blanks out in the way that a person who suddenly starts screaming in the middle of a crowded street clears a space. He began talking about the man he'd killed, and explained that when he ran off he'd had a revelation—he insisted on the word "revelation" and repeated it—and that he'd seen the world blanked out by sheets of snow. Wite had started talking when I mentioned the dead woman and the live baby, and he was explaining to me in his fashion. Wite said nothing more about it. I was made to understand somehow that he would answer no more questions about it, and say nothing more.

While Wite and I were traveling to the border, we always used graveyards for hiding, and we were everywhere sheltered by gravediggers, but like all spirit-eaters we had spent a great deal of time in cemeteries. Death does clear the necessary space for life. Life proceeds in sequence, and it requires death to clear each step, and the spirit-eaters are clear; they do the clearing. Because they are blank, they are able to volatilize their blankness and make it poison, make it an acid. Wite had been driven out into the woods and toward his own country by this thought of an infinite and volatile blank. I imagined it as he did, like a sheet of snow.

Wite and I fled toward Heipacth together, we were almost always together during this time, and I remember that, in some way, I was starting to feel my own life. I remember how ghostly my own life seemed to me. The peace of the graveyard made me feel it like a steady insistent rain in my body. Wite said that he felt not so much his life as what was left of his life like a colony of ants endlessly at work in every part of his body—this was typical of the way Wite generally expressed himself, although I can't reduce this to a principle, actually I won't reduce it to a principle. Wite spoke briefly of his life and I thought about and felt mine, and now I feel my life bleeding out of me in steadily diminishing pulses onto this page. When my body fails me altogether, at last, the spirits will devour me, or Wite will, so that I imagine I will fall into his infinite sheet of snow. I don't imagine however that it will make much difference, even to me, although I am starting to make plans, I'm starting even now to carry out little thought experiments, as I glimpse my dying day ahead. There are small ideas coming to me gradually; you'll hear of them by and by.

Once, when Wite and I were drawing close to the border, we stopped at another cemetery; we had stopped at so many cemeteries our trip was turning into one continuous cemetery laid out like a stripe from the capital to the border. The gravedigger had hidden us in an empty stone cottage on the forest border of the cemetery. We sat in there, and Wite finally explained to me that he was returning to his so-called native land to see his cousin, who was an aristocrat. I had been expecting something like this, but he had never told me his plans until then. Wite planned to kill himself after he saw her—somehow I had expected this as well, at least I don't remember being surprised. Wite was from Heipacth, and very few people understand that Heipas, as they call themselves, cannot die outside Heipacth. If a Heipa is mortally injured, or felled by an illness, or by the effects of age, outside the boundaries Heipacth, and these boundaries are not at all clear and distinct, he will lie dying indefinitely; or, until his body is returned to Heipacth. Even over a space of years, there was no telling how long a Heipa could lie dying outside Heipacth. Heipas seldom travel alone for this reason. They must return to Heipacth or lie dying forever—imagine that! They never go to sea. I imagine lying here on my prison floor until the stones crumble beneath me. Wite plainly told me that he intended to kill himself after meeting with his cousin in Heipacth. I didn't ask why. I didn't make it a practice to bother him with impertinent questions and I virtually never could come up with any that didn't seem impertinent after a moment or two of reflection. Life for a soul burner is nothing but unease, not to say pain, and it only gets worse; there's no improving it; after a certain point that seems to pass almost at once, in some cases perhaps before the spirit-eater becomes a soul burner, the soul burner is a lost cause. Wite was clearly a lost cause from the beginning. On the other side of death, there is a kind of other life waiting for strong soul burners, the soul burner can escape into death in his own way—this is something that can't be described, it bears only a slight similarity to, for example, the case of a hopeless invalid who kills himself. It can't be said, what death is for a soul burner. Almost all soul burners kill themselves; a soul burner finds greater suffering in his body every day, wakes up with a kind of disappointment to find his arms and legs trailing on all sides. At least, this is what I believe to be true. I had been expecting something like this from Wite.

If I go on and on, if I seem to want to talk forever, let me remind you that I fled with Wite for weeks; we were together constantly, and whenever we were together I felt him hammering at me, volatilizing me, beating my own hatreds out of the brush—my hatred for the people who were at every moment racing towards us like so many arrows, and for the people who had sent them after us. I held everyone responsible, and I still do now. Then, and for most of my life, I had nothing to say to anyone. Now that I'm sure to die in the next few days, in such a short time, I find I have everything to say.

Wite held no one responsible, he took all responsibility on himself. He had been universally adored from the first days of his life. He told me that his childhood had been filled with nothing but love. Wite had been encouraged in every enterprise, his family had thought him very "enter-prising." Wite said that people had thought the world of his intelligence and talent, and that he had been given every opportunity. Wite was still a young man then. He had never suffered, except for little things. All his sufferings had been on a petty scale, only little things. Now that I can do nothing but think, it seems to me that the most trivial pains are more important than the tragedies; they cause the most unbearable despera-tion; they gradually build up into a suffocating mass. Everywhere you go you will see people very slowly suffocating under the pressure from this mass of little pains, having the life squeezed out of them every day by this suffocating mass, suffering that's all the more intense for being worthless, incommunicable. Wite said that he had been suffocated until the moment he had, arbitrarily and randomly, murdered. He insisted that I understand he had felt no special resentment toward the man he killed, that man had vanished the moment he died, that man had no presence for Wite; he felt no guilt, he could have just as easily saved that man's life, given his own life for that man, as killed him, and, when he said this, I could tell that Wite was not denying a guilty conscience to me, he was telling me that he had no conscience—he knew that I in particular had to understand that. Wite had killed the smoker absent-mindedly, and he had killed Prince Eskellde the same way.

I had been filled with nothing but bad thoughts for years, and I had done nothing at all about them. I lived as if my every thought and feel-ing hadn't existed. Wite had not only refused to deny himself even the smallest act of selfishness, regardless of its consequences, he had refused for no reason at all, while I had plenty of reasons, my entire life was my reason! Of course, I say this knowing how bad it sounds; I say it because it sounds bad. when I saw Wite kill Prince Eskellde, I hadn't done anything at all to stop it happening, and this was the first selfish thing I had ever done. Or perhaps it wasn't, I might have been simply too surprised to act. This testament is the last selfish thing I'll do, unless dying is selfish. Can I act selfishly after all? Suddenly I'm unsure. Wite's plan to commit suicide was absolutely selfish, it was the most selfish thing he could possibly have done, his suicide had nothing to do with "killing himself." Wite's suicide was precisely his way of avoiding "killing himself." Actually I suppose it's very common for people to kill themselves to avoid dying, it's the most common thing. They inure themselves to death by taking it in small doses. Spirit-eaters do this professionally, they make a profession out of it. Wite was planning to take it still farther, as I was to learn; he planned to put it into effect in a wholly novel way. I can't say this any more clearly—he planned actually to do it. He had the most inventive plan, a very creative plan. When he told me, briefly, without the slightest detail, that he intended to kill himself, I knew that I would do everything I could to help him in the same way that I knew when I saw him in the clearing that I would not shoot him, that I would help him to escape instead, and that I was still helping him to escape. Wite's suicide was the final step of his escape. But he had to reach Heipacth first, and he wanted to see his cousin.

The night before we crossed the border, we stayed in an empty grave-digger's shed, by the treeline. I remember the sound of the wind crashing through the trees made me feel exhausted and glad to be inside, but Wite was nervous. He stood at one of the tiny windows and stared out at the sky, which had been scoured clear by the wind. I lay down and watched him standing motionless at the window. Later, still in the middle of the night, I woke suddenly in a panic, having just then come awake out of a very deep sleep. I was completely asleep, I mean as asleep as I have ever been, but even in the midst of this total sleep I had felt something terrifying and been jerked awake—I had been hearing a low, continuous sound that had seemed to me, as I slept, like something invading the shed. I was completely disoriented for a few minutes. My senses were overlapped and I had to untangle them. Finally I could tell that the sound was coming from Wite, that he was moaning in his sleep. His mouth was open and a cry was quietly pouring out of it. I think I sat there staring for some time without knowing what to do, I had wondered if I ought to go outside, I actually felt embarrassed. Then Wite snapped upright and he screamed, his body blazed and he threw his arms up in front of his face, he lunged forward thrusting his hands ahead of him, diving at the wall. His hands disappeared into the stones of the wall and exploded knocking me back as if I'd been struck in the chest with a mallet. I had seen flame in his fingers as he'd lunged forward and I had seen the stones shiver into powder when his hands sank into them. The windows broke too—I had to sit still and stop my whirling head; when I could manage to look around I saw that the shed had burst open on one side, the wall had been knocked out and there was a great ragged hole there. I scrambled out through the hole in the wall without thinking, or at most I was afraid the roof would cave in on me.

I got outside into the open air and a blast of wind brought me to my senses. I began to look for Wite. He had shot out of the shed when the wall flew apart and torn through the high grass along the treeline. A few moments later I found him, lying in the grass, which was thrashing back and forth over his body. He was lying on his back and convulsing, his spine was scissoring off the ground driving his head down into the earth below him and his arms and legs alternately jerked and went rigid; his eyes were gaping wide staring up at the sky and his mouth was stretched, he was gasping and taking deep frantic breaths. He appeared to be struggling beneath an immense weight. As I came up to him, his hands shot out at the sky, and they snapped shut on empty air. He did this several times, and when I leaned over him to try to help, he pushed me off awkwardly and his breathing became more ragged and desperate. I sat back and gave him air, and he continued to writhe on the ground for a while. For some reason I found it calming to watch him. His breathing eventually slowed and he stopped stabbing the air with his arms. His eyes remained fixed on the sky, which was absolutely clear. Then, all of a sudden, Wite was fine. He stood up and walked back to the shed, without speaking to me, and looked at the ruined wall for a few minutes. He seemed prepared to go back inside, then he turned and walked over to the horses, lying down in the roots of a tree, and went to sleep. I couldn't bring myself to go back into the shed either, and so I lay down in the grass where I was.

Later, Wite explained that he had had a nightmare in his hands. He dreamt that ghosts were trying to pull him down into the ground, that they were trying to crush him under the shed, and that he needed to get out into the open air again.

CHAPTER FOUR

———

Now I want nothing but water. After I don't know how many days, wasting my little strength trying to explain to them that I don't want them to bring me any more food, no food of any kind, today they left me only a pitcher of water. I drained it all at once and immediately regretted it, was too weak to ask for more. Now it strikes me as ridiculous, contemptible of me not to ask for more. They bring me pitchers of water and I drain them all at once, and it drains away and disappears into my body without a trace, while my brow is forever hotter and drier, my throat is forever hotter and drier. Wite was revolted by food and digestion, and as spirit-eaters we both know better than anyone, we have as much to do with dead bodies as gravediggers do. When examined as an object, the human body is insanely complicated, like a dream made concrete, assembled from the most unwholesome things imaginable. Even the nerves are revolting to hold in your hand. But here my nerves, as brittle as glass, are yet perverse enough to drag my ponderous body up, when I should have no more energy than is required to die, and compel me to *write*. I feel new energy when I begin to write, a surplus that is drained away as I write, but which leaves the principle, my body, untouched. But I could not prolong my life by prolonging my testament, because of course my story is my life. If I were inventing things, that might keep me alive. Without sleep, all the partitions fall out of time, the days and nights collapse together into a single beam of time from which I feel myself beginning to fall away already, by increments.

Wite and I entered Heipacth through a cleft rock, climbing up into Heipacth along a ravine. I had never left my country before and I found the air in Heipacth unwholesome, especially in the ravines, and in that ravine in particular. At its lowest point there was a narrow riverbed filled with stinking black muck that exhaled the most unwholesome air I've ever breathed. My uncle Heckler once told me that Heipacth was "poisoned," and now I know he had spoken as accurately as could be desired. I followed Wite along the riverbank as best I could. I remember watching his back. He rode with his head thrust forward and down, and his coat would be thrust up along his back so that the collar stood high up on his shoulders and his head was completely obscured by his back. I had to watch him closely because the few trees there were had grown so enormous that they almost completely blocked the sun. I could only keep my eyes on Wite's back, and the world turned into a tunnel. After a while I remember feeling that I couldn't tear my eyes away from Wite's back, that I would spend the next few hours staring at it. Then for the first time it occurred to me to be frightened of Wite. I stared at his back and I was suddenly terrified that he might *turn around and look at me*, and that instant I was certain that he inevitably would, and that I would be staring at him like I would stare in a *nightmare*, and then *he turned around and looked at me*. He turned his head just as if it was a *nightmare*. His face was the color of ice even in the total shadow of the ravine. It was unrecognizable. A sound was emanating from it, one that I had heard before, but which I cannot describe. It seemed to come from every direction, and affected me like a scream. Then he turned his head away, and all the while I had continued to follow him, even though it was impossible. It never occurred to me to run away, any more than it would have occurred to me to wake myself up from a nightmare, even to notice that it's a nightmare that I'm having. The most terrifying thing about a nightmare is precisely that you've forgotten you're dreaming. So I followed Wite into Heipacth. Only a few moments later we took our bearings in a clearing and I was able to look at Wite calmly; we were through that change.

For weeks after that, there was next to nothing to see but infinite forest and Wite's inconstant face. Once in Heipacth I noticed the horses were haggard and disheveled, that Wite and I were both covered with filth and hanging in pieces. We followed the courses of brooks into Heipacth and slept at random intervals on their banks, sometimes down in the rushes, on sandbanks narrow enough for one man to lie sideways, with his feet curled, and we would wake with our hands trailing in cold water, turning to mush. I would knock my numb hands against rocks to restore the feeling. My clothes never dried out and smelled of mold. Wite would drive his horse unrelentingly, forever redirecting it, pointing its head away from the mountains and down into the woods again. He hardly ever spoke—he drove on toward his cousin's place with dire impatience and unwavering confidence in his powers of navigation. The sky was always grey, and the moment immediately preceding sunrise and following sunset, when the air fluoresces blue, seemed prolonged, especially deep among the trees— the raw cold of that fluorescence always gave me a feeling of insomnia, no matter how much or how little sleep I might have had. We plunged headlong almost every waking moment, and Wite collapsed from exhaustion and sickness a number of times along the way. He was deteriorating, his body was rejecting him. There were no signs of human habitation, although Wite assured me we passed close by several well-hidden Heipa towns; they communicated with each other along massive branches in the forest canopy, woven together to form suspended avenues and aquaducts, and they lived down inside the more massive trees, and in burrows underground. They all lived fathoms underground.

Wite was my entire society then, really no society of any kind. I chose him to the exclusion of everyone else. But through him I met his cousin Tzdze, and she became the other *pole star* for me; she lived removed from the cities, and I loved her as much as I loved Wite. I never loved Wite; but I did love Tzdze. If you weren't expecting confessions of love, you shouldn't forget you know absolutely nothing about me and have no business to expect anything, this or that, from me. You've had entirely too much time in which to put out your fine phrases. Now you will have to listen to mine and without jumping to conclusions or trying to fit together what I say, or deciding in advance what it's all about. Futility is what it's about. I have absolutely nothing whatever to do with that "all" in your "what it's all about," that's the all you've crept under but it isn't mine. Because of them, Tzdze on the one side, and Wite on the other, I was finally able to cut myself off from cities and societies and what you would expect—from you, to put it in a word. I emphasize that I took perverse and willfull pleasure in cutting those bonds to you, that I certainly felt Wite's deadly altitude sinking its shadowy roots into me as I turned finally away, and I was ecstatic, I was filled with genuinely savage ecstasy to feel that canker sinking into my heart at last, to see the faces of that handful of friends and colleagues in my mind and to say no to them—finally no. For all your endless good qualities and the goodness of your hearts, and I was constantly meeting good-hearted people, and perhaps even partially because of that good-heartedness, just for the perversity of rejecting such good-heartedness, I will turn aside from you, and if you try to interfere with me no matter what your intentions you will become an enemy. What a fierce, tonic joy it is to have enemies! I turned away once and for all, so many times, and I won't stop turning, not ever, even after the end. When I followed Wite into the forests and resolved to do everything in my power to help him escape, to fulfill his plans no matter what, I made him the full scope and set of my society, which was no society, and in all its viciousness and hatefulness, the bitterness and poisonedness of this decision, I took the greatest possible pleasure. By reducing myself in this way, in the most unconditional and unhealthy way, I suddenly was content, even in the muck and confusions. I knew Wite wanted to destroy those cities, that he was their annihilating opposite, and now I was a part of him, already a part of him and his plan. I was an invaluable element in his plan and in his opposition to the cities, and I will be honest for once and confess—this testament is a boast, I'm gloating over all of *you* for once—precisely because I have no right to, precisely because I stole that right for myself. He pulled me along at his speed, ever increasing speed, until suddenly we passed through a yew hedge and Tzdze's house appeared in front of me, all balconies and buttresses, filling my vision, covered with brass tusks, and I could see spirits teeming thickly there, screaming to each other, these invisible-intangible tropical birds, bright visible and audible to Wite and me. We rode directly into the courtyard. I had never been welcomed at a house before.

But Wite, when he came through the door into the courtyard and brought his horse up short, when he looked up at the walls and the mountain towering overhead . . . I saw his face split again as if it was about to burst, and I felt I was about to burst, we both were bursting just being there, within the walls of Tzdze's house, with the mountain towering overhead—the house recognized Wite, and what's more, it recognized *me*! Both Wite and I, neither of us had ever been recognized anywhere, we had no place anywhere, but now suddenly Tzdze's house recognized us. Don't expect any explanation. Let explanation rot and crumble away to dust and less than dust. Even in the forest, where we had been more free than ever, where we were at liberty to be welcome there, we had never been recognized. In the forest we take our places wherever we want, there's nothing to prevent us, we belong there but nothing's been done to admit us, nothing has been done to us. At Tzdze's house, Wite and I instantly had our place, and we were both ready to die, we had never felt anything like this before. I started shaking. Wite was off his horse already, out of breath, his head flashing back and forth, looking. A moment later he saw Tzdze, who had come to the balcony overhead and was looking down at us, along with her younger sister. Except for the difference in age, Tzdze and her younger sister looked exactly alike. I could see their white faces, dark hair and dark eyes, and their small hands on the balustrade, as they both looked straight down at us, one head lower than the other. Wite and his cousin looked at each other for a long time. I remember watching them. One of a pair of gardeners was asking me questions in Heipa, and I suppose I said something to them in Alak, they took the horses to the stables. We had appeared unexpectedly, in shocking condition, but they, with perfect graciousness, simply led our horses to the stables. Another pair of house servants met us at the rear door and took us inside. All the while I imagined Tzdze was still standing on the balcony with her sister.

I didn't meet Tzdze until later, and I assume Wite went to speak with her in private first. I was left with nothing to do, having been deserted by both of them—but Tzdze's house was something like them both, and there were many times I could very easily convince myself that I felt them with me. Without any ceremony at all, I was conveyed to a room, which was *my room*. As if it had been waiting for me all my life. My room was small with disproportionately large windows, which were filled with light but deeply recessed. I remember being dazzled as I first entered it from the darkness of the hall. The house was tenanted by countless servants. I saw different persons every time I looked out of my windows or left my room. But the house was always perfectly quiet—at most there would be whispering or very light footfalls. There were no common meals—from that point on I no longer ate with Wite, nor did I eat at first with Tzdze or her sister, or in any company during my stay there. The food was brought to my room. I mention this to explain that there were no chimes used to announce meals. The only chime in the house belonged to an enormous clock built into the walls on the ground floor, which rang every hour with a low, dull, monotonous thudding. It had a ponderously long, heavy pendulum that swung over a great distance. The ticking was audible through the walls and floors throughout the house. I remember sleeping there in Tzdze's house more deeply than I've ever slept. I would fall asleep almost instantly and sleep for the most part without dreaming, without waking, without moving, until morning, when I would revive quietly, without feeling either tired or refreshed. I would wake up feeling as if no time had passed, or rather, that the intervening time had been removed somehow, without altering the fact that my body had slept. Now that I can't sleep at all I find it impossible to forget the way I slept at Tzdze's house.

I met Tzdze that night, and only briefly. I had gone to my room and cleaned myself up. There was a bath drawn for me across the hall, and I washed myself with great pleasure. I walked back to my room, across the hall and put on the clothes I found for me in my room. Doing these homely things I felt like I was playing. The servants appeared only when they were required, otherwise I never saw them unless they were just leaving the room, having just finished whatever it was they were doing. As I said, the house was full of servants. I couldn't imagine there was that much to do, but everything there was spotless, in perfect working order, with not a single squeaking hinge or loose board. The presence of the servants filled the house with tension. Outside of my room, every trace that I left behind was instantly erased. They all seemed to me to have very honest, very cold faces, and I wonder now what sort of beings they were. They were nothing like people at all. After I had made myself presentable, as presentable as I could be, which must have been pretty bad all the same, I was at liberty to look around the house. The air in the house was exceptionally good—it was like the air in libraries. There were many rooms, most of them small, most of them sealed and unused for years, but the air was everywhere the same, not stale. There was no dust. Most of the house was dark. In those rooms that Tzdze frequented the walls were covered with polished brass screens shaped like trellises of vines and flowers, and here and there one of the blossoms would be made of either extremely thin porcelain, glass, or crystal perhaps, and there would be a place for a light inside. The floors were made of polished wood, smooth and red, red enough to appear black, and reflecting. Tzdze's taste was perfect. I was going through the house when a servant found me and brought me up to introduce me to Tzdze. She was in one of the upstairs rooms, also decorated with brass vines and flowers, and some of these were lit up as I described. The resulting light was very soft.

The image of Tzdze and Wite as I saw them together when I entered the room recurs to me so often that I find it hard to imagine seeing it for the first time. Wite was standing in one of the corners, by the window, which was high and small, with faint moonlight on his face. Tzdze was sitting in the middle of the room, her chair was turned halfway to face Wite, her face was in half-profile. She was beautifully dressed and perfectly erect in her chair. There was a table beside her chair, with a light that shone on her face. She was looking at Wite in an attitude of expectation, and she was sitting bolt upright, with a stern expression, looking very young and strong, and her features stood out so sharply they appeared to be carved in the air. She turned her attention to me as I came in and she introduced herself politely. I don't remember what I said, except that I told her my name. My voice sounded so idiotic that I decided to say as little as politeness would permit. She told me she wanted to thank me for her own sake, and on Wite's behalf. She didn't look at Wite at any time after I came in. He stood motionless in the corner. I seem to recall his pale face hovering in the corner of my eye. Tzdze said that she wanted me to stay with her as her guest and to promise to give her whatever help she might ask, and I agreed. It's possible that was the moment I understood that I never wanted to leave. At that moment I thought Tzdze was asking me somehow to help her cousin kill himself, and that she had decided to help Wite to kill himself as he had planned. I assumed Wite had explained to her why he had come and what he planned to do, and that she was prepared to help. I had hardly been able to think about it, I had no ideas—but my head was full of nonsense, of ridiculous and presumptuous words, and I didn't want to earn her contempt by using them. My head was all whirling and I was completely unprepared to speak, nevertheless, I think I said something absurd like "I understand." Under circumstances like these "I understand" is always a piece of stupidity or cowardice, I don't know what it is but it's always a lie or a confusion, no one can "understand." Tzdze's attention was so intense that I began to feel exhausted. She noticed and said "You seem tired." I think I waved my hands somehow. She said "Well, then, good-night." I said good-night to her, and then to Wite, and left.

It was only when I awoke the next morning, in my room, in that house, that the full force of my first impression struck me, that the atmosphere of Tzdze's house was an atmosphere that adhered to Tzdze and Wite and which emanated from them both. I had lived in the city most of my life, and as I looked back from the bed in which I lay, as I do now in my prison cell, everything about the life I had led before I joined the hunting party, especially my life with my wife, none of it made any sense to me from the point of view of Tzdze's house, nor could I understand how I came to be there. My wife's death was a terrible loss to me in every way. I have lied, saying I won't speak about my wife. My memory of her is sealed with the kind of pain that doesn't yield anything to learn or any dignity. I married her out of pain, lived with her in pain, and when she died I suffered again, always the same. When my son turned on me and shouted in my face, then I felt something like amazement, although it was only the occasion that surprised me, not the attack, which I had expected, which, in a way, I had been enduring continuously for years. But when he left, and I was completely abandoned, I felt only the urge to laugh, although not to laugh *uproariously*. I only shrugged it off; it was all too pitiful not to be funny. In my work I was a success, and I felt my accomplishments only made my continuing to live any life more perverse. Only my resignation, which by then must have been almost complete, made it possible for me to enjoy anything. Then, of all possible times, I am surprised by this miracle, waking up in Tzdze's house!

I never permitted myself any sentimentality, I despised everyone and was hated for it, I was paid in kind and I owe nothing, nor am I owed anything. I was no slave—I succeeded because I enjoyed betraying my countrymen to the Alaks, do you see that? And because I knew I was making the Alaks more hateful to my countrymen by yielding so many up to them. I hated the Alaks as intensely as I hated the vicious men and shrewish women of my own so-called country. Wite and Tzdze were my own kind. I loved *them* both. I was prepared to make them any sacrifice, all kinds of worthless, frantic offerings. When I went to the window, I saw Tzdze on one of the balconies below mine, which was set enough forward that I could see its far edge. Tzdze flashed past in an instant, from left to right, and the shock it gave me held me by the window for a long time. Tzdze emitted a single note that made the house ring; an infinitely extended, inhumanly pure note shone from her.

The next day, Wite gave me a tour of the grounds. I'm sure he'd wanted to go alone, but he was weak that day and leaned on my shoulder several times. Even with me he was practically alone. I could sense the terrible, ghostly strain he was under; his face was even more bloodless and rigid than usual, and he had a stricken expression. We walked together through the grounds like a pair of condemned prisoners, and he would look up again and again to the mountain that loomed over the estate, at whose feet the estate was. The mountain rose up directly from the ground along the back border of the estate. In particular, I noticed Wite would glance again and again at a small stone outbuilding high up the slope. It was hard to describe, looking like a small, isolated porch with a heavy, curved roof. When Wite finally spoke, it was to tell me that this small building was the place he had chosen to die. He was looking up to it as he said this to me, with dread. I asked him if I could stay, and he replied that I could as far as he was concerned but that I would need to ask Tzdze for her consent. Although he didn't entirely belong there, it seemed impossible to imagine Wite coming to rest anywhere else but there. Now that we had come to rest, Wite seemed paralyzed. Neither he nor I had anywhere left to go or any reason to leave, and so we inevitably stayed. While we were touring the grounds, Wite asked me questions about the Alaks and the spirit-eaters, about investigations. I had no idea whether he was interested or not, but he listened with the same agitated, stricken expression I had seen on his face before. I told him what I could, and his questions reminded me of a time when I had been out of the city for a few days. When I had returned, I had heard that a group of my so-called countrymen, partisans, had been arrested for the usual crimes and were sentenced to die. In retaliation, their comrades had kidnapped a number of Alak representatives, including the sister-in-law of one of my supervisors. She was my wife's closest friend, one of the only people who ever visited us, and she was pregnant at the time. The magistrate had ordered the execution to proceed, and the hostages were discovered drowned the same day. I was there watching as they were pulled from the water—my supervisor and his brother were there, and I remember his brother collapsed when they pulled his wife out. I went over and looked at her. I asked her where she had been and she told me, and I directed them to a house several streets over. This was the only time I had ever really wielded power—I told them where to go; I had worked with this particular supervisor for years and he, from a distance, knew precisely what I could be depended upon to do. As it happens, he didn't survive long after. Under his instructions, the men followed me to the house—the partisans were packing their things into a cart in the street, tossing stuff down from the upstairs windows. They panicked when we appeared, and I suppose this convinced the soldiers; they surrounded the house and started tearing it apart with axes and bars. Moments later they were dragging partisans out of the house and tossing them into a sort of cage on wheels, banging on the bars on all sides to keep the prisoners heaped up in the center of the cage, the partisans inside cringed and wailed as if they were being beaten themselves. One of the two ringleaders had not been found inside, and I was asked to go in and ask the spirits—of that I will only say that they didn't know, and that I ate them all within a few minutes. Then a soldier rushed up to me and brought me around to the lot behind the house. I heard screams. The first soldier through the back door of the house had fallen through a hole in the floor, and broken his leg horribly. They had dragged him out into the yard. The foot and lower part of the calf were almost at a right angle to the rest of his leg, his blood was gushing out onto the ground. I was disgusted. I was horrified at his pain. I was disgusted *and* I was horrified at his pain. I had just blanked the house of spirits, I was filled with their animation, so I seized his leg in my hands. The bone slid immediately back under the skin and knitted together, and the muscles over it, the blood stopped coming out, the skin closed, and his leg was restored. As his screaming stopped in abrupt surprise I was suddenly overcome with fury at the ringleaders of this idiotic band of so-called patriots, for all their childish destruction and for lowering me to the task of cleaning up after them, for forcing me to witness this disgusting spectacle and take part in it, for killing my wife's friend (the supervisor's sister-in-law) notwithstanding how little she meant to me, and for killing her in the name of the pettiest and most absurd of causes, so I simply demanded of myself the location of that other of the two ringleaders, the one who had not been found, and suddenly I received a vivid impression.

I told the lieutenant and he immediately sent word to the adjutant. A number of men were sent off with me to find the other ringleader, with the understanding that another group of armed men dispatched by the adjutant himself would join us on the way. Now I was mustering forces, I was the one setting large operations in motion, of all people! Of all people, now I'm in charge of bringing in a criminal, with dozens of men at my disposal! I pointed them to the partisans and now I was leading them to fetch out the one remaining man, and, when I did, I would be recognized as the sole author of this triumph. My impulse then was to lead them around in circles, then abandon the search. I had been away when all of this started, and now I reappear and fix everything, restore order—even now I can't get over it, imagine me "restoring order!" I was glad to do it, too, I wanted to do it. My hatred for them overcame my hatred for the Alak representatives who used me. Now I understand how these abominable cities keep going, how they can get even someone like me into the act, when they offer the victim his chance to be a torturer himself. I led armed men to the top of the street, where the adjutant's group met us, and there was a minister with them, who so to speak took over from me. When I saw the minister I knew that the adjutant planned to "make an example" of the second of the ringleaders and I felt both satisfied and terribly distressed. The soldiers surrounded the house and knocked on the door—I instantly "knew" it was empty, except for him, and the minister knew it too. The minister simply plunged its two front paws through the door and seized both sides of the jamb, tearing them out and much of the wall as well. The opening it had made was still too small, and it seized one of the posts that supported the house's frame and wrenched it out of place, breaking it in two. The soldiers fell back and the upper eaves of the house collapsed inward, dropping several heavy timbers across the minister's back. I heard a cry almost in the same moment and saw a figure in the alley beside the house—he had just leapt out a window. The minister lunged forward and seized him, then bounded out into the street again. It brought the second ringleader out of the alley, holding him unharmed and wailing in one of its middle hands. It held him up, so that the mob that had gathered could see him. I watched its blank, inhuman face, with lidless protruding eyes that saw in all directions, and this terrified me and attracted me in exactly the same way that Wite terrifies and attracts me. It dropped the second ringleader into the street and tore him to bits in an instant, without spilling a drop of blood, for it all drained out across its skin and boiled immediately away into an invisible cloud of red steam. In the blink of an eye there was nothing left of the second ringleader but a pile of fragments, as clean and dry as scraps of cloth or dead leaves.

I told Wite this story, but he seemed already far beyond paying me any attention. Will you believe me when I tell you that it was only then that I first realized he was a murderer? He had killed at least a dozen people. He had killed Prince Eskellde in front of me. He had murdered someone right in front of me but it was only now that I thought of him, speculatively, as a murderer. He had never seemed like a murderer to me before, and the people he killed seemed to have been killed by a natural disaster. I had thought of him as a force of nature, and now I was his accomplice. None of this had occurred to me until I had told him this story—during our flight together I never thought about it. I knew the Alaks, I had participated in their investigations and worked with their magistrates. I knew it was genuinely impossible that they would fail to find Wite. They would set their sights, with clear and unclouded eyes, on his trail, and would follow him until they brought him back. They certainly couldn't permit the man who murdered Prince Eskellde to go free, but, even if Wite had killed only people of no particular importance, the Alaks would never tolerate him, would spare no difficulty in finding him, would harry him all his life. The Alaks established order. From the ancient days of their first kingdoms they reached out with the intention of embracing everyone they met as an Alak; they could not imagine a human being who was not an Alak—Wite, to them, was either an Alak in need of correction, or something not human. Regardless of what he was to them, and I want to stress that he could never be an object of their hatred, for they hated nobody, they would not rest until he was accounted for somehow. They wanted less to punish him than to account for him. It was a miracle they had not already found us. The longer we remained at Tzdze's, and we were not going anywhere, the more likely it was that they would find us. Inevitably, they would find us. I had no idea what to expect when they arrived, and I vaguely wondered what they would make of me as Wite's accomplice. I assumed they thought I was dead. I had taken responsibility for Wite from the first, and I felt even more strongly my responsibility to him then. His knees buckled under him and he fell down on the grass, coughing or retching, and I immediately knelt beside him and took his shoulders in my hands. He was trembling uncontrollably. He seemed completely powerless, mortally sick.

I felt responsible for him. I still wanted to help him, but was I going to help him kill himself? He was thoroughly poisoned with spite, and how could I help someone like that? But I never doubted that I would stay with him to the last, and that I would suffer when it was over, and that until then he would suffer much worse and that I would have to give him what meagre help I could. If they came and shot at him, I thought then that I would selflessly shield him with my body, step forward completely without fear and without offering harm to anyone, just to prevent a bullet from reaching him and thus give him another moment of life to draw breath in. I was full of silly ideas, I hardly knew who it was I walked next to! If he decided to end his own life, that would be an enigma to me. All this dawned on me as I knelt down beside him and held his shoulders.

I want to end this chapter neatly for you, but I've run out of things to say. These "chapters" are nonsense, they tidy up messy things, but it's important that the story be clear, and I promise I'm telling everything honestly.

CHAPTER FIVE

———

After I brought Wite back inside I was called to meet Tzdze. I can't move any faster than this and I can't skip anything, and I have no choice. I would have to write everything out in this way no matter what, no matter whether I wanted to or not, this is a testament, I must write it this way. I do not have the audacity to try to claim this is all voluntary and a gesture of my own freedom, or as an act of my will at all, properly understood. My arms rise from my sides and I sit up, and my hands pull me across the room to the table, and I begin to write, still sleeping, still delirious, almost not here at all, exhausted, completely worn out. I act mechanically, powerlessly, without will, but not in apathy, burned up as I am, failing as I am, there is no apathy. Back then I had no intention, no thought, of writing about any of this, the idea would have offended me then. I'm offending as I write this, but I have been granted immunity, I offend on someone else's behalf, and I am condemned and outside punishment already.

I was summoned to Tzdze's sitting room, which was long and had many windows low to the floor. The ceiling was also low, but not so low as to make it necessary for me to bow my head, although I did bow my head as I entered. There was a large table in the middle of the room, set lengthwise in the center, and Tzdze was sitting on the other side, facing me, in the middle of the table. Her hands were on her chair's arms. There was another chair on my side of the table, opposite her, and there was a backgammon set lying open on the table in front of her. Tzdze sternly asked me if I would play backgammon with her, and I think I said "all right." I remember how weak my voice was in her presence, and that the room was silent. We started playing. Tzdze was dressed in white. I wonder how I'll do, describing Tzdze? Tzdze was dressed in white, and her arms moved mechanically across the board, beating me. Presently, I remember, her sister came in and sat down behind her in a beautifully embroidered armchair, and began doing needlepoint. I could hear her breath in her nostrils, I can hear it right now. Tzdze won and asked me to play again, and we started playing backgammon again. She played expertly. I was distracted at first but I began playing more seriously as the second game started. I had played backgammon with my wife and with some of the apostates who would come to visit, sometimes every day. We would all sit together without saying anything to each other, anything but bare and plain things, and we would eat peanuts soaked in coffee and drink black tea. We would be drenched in sweat, drinking glass after glass of tea, brewing more, drinking more, until we were steaming ourselves, and our play would get correspondingly faster. My wife and I never drank tea as compulsively when we would play in the evening. My wife liked to drink red wine afterward, to help her sleep. She would usually throw her hands up and forfeit the game to me, and silently clear away the tea things and the board. Then she would bring in a glass of wine and drink it by the window while I would lock up the house. What have I been saying? Tzdze's sister left the room and came back, came and went like a pendulum. I would see her face out of the corner of my eye, swinging back into the room. Tzdze beat me again and immediately set the board up again, without asking me if I wanted to play again, and we began to play again. She was looking sternly at the board and her lips were compressed. I thought she was disgusted at having beaten me so easily. Her sister left the room. By now I was able to concentrate. Tzdze was losing. Her arms swung back and forth over the board as she moved her pieces, gracefully, efficiently, precisely. I saw the expression on her face grow more relaxed while becoming more concentrated. In the next room her sister began playing something quietly on a piano. I didn't recognize the piece. I know nothing about music and never learned to play or sing, unlike most apostates. My wife played guitar beautifully, and she also sang well, well enough for plain music. She would play for me on nights when we didn't feel like backgammon, and sometimes she would sing, and when she got tired I would read to her. I always enjoyed listening to her. I felt closest to her when she would play and sing. Now Tzdze's sister was playing very quietly in the next room. Tzdze took no notice and continued playing. I beat Tzdze. She seemed satisfied and excused herself. I remained sitting at the table until her sister finished her piece and the music subsided.

Wite spent days either in his room or in the stone outbuilding; if he wasn't to be found in his room, he would be in the outbuilding, which was most often the case. Generally I did not visit his room, nor could I imagine him inhabiting it. Wite was not to be given a room. But from the start the stone outbuilding was his, as if he'd brought it with him. During this time his health declined, and the few times I saw him I was shocked at how *deathly ill* he looked. I never recognized Wite when I saw him. As I think about it now I'm certain Wite was spending his nights up in the stone outbuilding and that it was ruining his health, which was already bad. He avoided me completely. Tzdze may have seen him during this time, but he had nothing to do with me and said little to me, and Tzdze almost never spoke to me about him. Tzdze and I now played backgammon together every night after dinner, with little conversation. The one occasion she did mention Wite, she was speaking with her sister, whose name was Xchte, and I remember she said Wite looked hounded. Apart from remarking to Xchte that Wite looked hounded Tzdze never said anything about him during these games, and Tzdze never said anything about him to me directly during these games. When we spoke at all, apart from the essentials which were reduced by Tzdze's mere presence to the bare minimum, it was usually about me. When I talked about myself in response to Tzdze's questions, I could hear the words hit the air woodenly, and I knew that Tzdze questioned me about myself because to hear me speak about myself is to hear only a modulation of the quiet of empty rooms and everyday things. Later on I realized that she heard every word I said and every *thing* I said, but at the time I thought that Tzdze bade me speak to be her music box, for the plain and unengaging way I talked.

Tzdze asked me about my wife. I told her that our marriage had been arranged by the other apostates in the capital. We met each other a number of times by only apparent coincidence. Neither of us was aware at the time that these coincidences were arranged by the apostates. This was usual, I told Tzdze. At the time I had just recovered from a long illness that had confined me to bed for weeks, only to discover that there was no work for me. I killed time by going into the country, came back depressed and nearly dying of boredom, and found there was still no work. During my illness my days had become completely formless, and afterward the lack of work left me with no external order, and I was unable to bring myself under discipline again. During that period I lost every day, and I was dying of boredom. She, my future wife, appeared again and again and eventually we noticed each other and very soon she was indispensable to me. She was almost immediately indispensable to me. We were mutually indispensable in almost no time, we went everywhere together and worked precisely together. Tzdze went on asking me about my wife. I only said that, shortly after my wife and I met, suddenly I was working every waking moment for weeks without respite, and that she was essential to me during this time. I told Tzdze that I would have been worked to death if my wife hadn't immediately seen where she was needed and moved to help. I would most likely have died from all that work, and most likely I would have died willingly, I would have worked myself to death knowing full well right from the start, if she hadn't been there to help me. With her help I neither died nor wanted to die. She visited me every day and looked after the things I had no time to do but which were essential if I were simply to go on living. Eventually she decided we should get married, so that she could be there all the time, and that was how we came to get married. Tzdze asked about the wedding. I said that we had had neither the time nor the money for a wedding, and I of course had no relatives to invite—although I've always been horrified at the thought of a traditional wedding full of useless relatives who want to get their fingers in, meddle and intrude in the most appallingly shameless way. I've always been disgusted by weddings, they bring out absolutely the worst in everybody. Two people get married and suddenly it's everybody's business, when that should be the last thing it is, and everyone within a dozen miles comes barging in with their tongues hanging out and their eyes bulging out of their sockets—these being the same people who made life impossible in the first place, who did everything in their power to drive us apart and destroy whatever enervated feelings we had left, who nearly killed us both by their constant interference and complete disrespect for us, who now want us to congratulate them and admit them even further into our lives when they're trespassing unforgivably as it is. My wife had a few relations and friends and insisted on some small reception for them, but we were married with as little ceremony and as hastily and awkwardly as possible. When I imagine us getting married, even now, I start laughing and I can't stop. I laughed even then, and I laughed as I told Tzdze about it, and even she laughed. Tzdze laughed right along with me. My wife and I were married in a ridiculous, half-destroyed ceremony in the presence of strangers, and then we held the reception. While my wife had insisted on the reception, it was thrown for us by a friend of hers. I sat and made the best of it, and while my wife enjoyed her friends' company, she was already ailing from the first of many chronic illnesses. After a couple of hours she began to tire rapidly and then one day she lost consciousness. I heard the clatter of her fall in the next room. She recovered after a few days of rest, but not before I caught whatever it was she had, and ended up sick in bed myself. Neither of us was ever in entirely good health and we were constantly making each other sick. We never quarrelled, although we separated once, but we were forever making each other sick.

Tzdze asked me about children, and I replied that I had a son. Before Tzdze asked me about my son she told me that she had no intention of marrying, that Xchte would be the one to marry, and that Xchte's children would inherit the estate. After Tzdze said this she asked me about my son and I said only that I had always been against having children, because my wife's health was fragile and because I felt neither of us could possibly justify the absurdity of a child. Unfortunately she became pregnant, despite our really frantic efforts to avoid it, and nearly died giving birth to our son. He exhausted us both with his demands and we aged horribly during his childhood. He took up with native children right away and spent most of his time with them and their relatives, and when he was old enough he told us that he despised us, that we were traitors, and he ran away. Despite my best efforts I was unable to locate him for a long time, I didn't discover what had become of him until after my wife's death, but if I had managed to find him, he would never have returned to us. I don't know what I would have done had I traced him earlier. It was entirely for my wife's benefit that I searched and searched for him; I thought he was either foolish or right in his own way, by turns, and never missed him that much. Apparently he had disowned us utterly and vanished among the other natives. He may even have joined the partisans, that would have been entirely consistent. Even as a very young boy he was always ill at ease with us; he never understood us. When my wife died we had both already forgotten each other. Tzdze listened to all this with a level expression, and played backgammon with me.

Tzdze lived alone with her twin sister Xchte and her many servants with no need at all for anyone, although she certainly had the capacity for strong attachments to people. There was nothing for miles in the vicinity of the house. Servants would ride back and forth regularly for days at a time for supplies, and others would forage and hunt whatever they could in the forest. I have never eaten better food in my life. The food of Tzdze's estate was unique. Although I was thinking of Wite with great pain all the time, I ate Tzdze's food ravenously. I've always hated feeling filled up with food, but the food at Tzdze's house never sat heavily on me in any quantity. I ate ravenously there not only because the food was excellent and prepared with great care, but because I felt the strong property of this unique food was something of Tzdze's. From the first I belonged to Tzdze, and by eating as much as I did I felt I was becoming more properly hers. Tzdze invited me to take my meals with her. Wite never joined us, and evidently ate very little or not at all during this time, and we never discussed him. We said next to nothing to each other during meals, I know I didn't because I've always been self-conscious about talking and eating. I feel disgusting enough as it is without the worrying logistics of eating food.

We did most of our conversing as we played backgammon in the long second-storey gallery. Apart from the momentary glimpses of her that I caught during the day as I would wander through the house, I always saw Tzdze at a table. I would sit just to the left of the foot of the table as we ate, while she would sit at the head of the table. When we played backgammon we sat opposite each other in the center of the table, and I faced the windows. Tzdze appeared to live in total order. She made a habit of fighting herself at every turn, of (cruelly) correcting herself impersonally. Tzdze resembled Wite in this way—he had a blindness to everything that wasn't directly in front of him that I admired. I have always been at risk of dissipation, siphoned off in every direction at the whim of this or that bit of trivia, while Wite had a wholly linear life, linear and inclined. He had no choices and no freedom, and there was never a question as to how he would end, there was nothing to choose, the only test he faced was a test of endurance, to carry on through to the end without stopping short. Tzdze's life was even more compressed, into a single point, but an infinitely rich and eternal point. It was from out of this point that Tzdze played backgammon with me.

Wite was always alone, I could never find him, I all but ceased to exist for him at that time I'm sure, and when I wasn't playing backgammon with Tzdze I would spend my time idling, wandering at random through the house while my head would fill itself with worthless thoughts. Tzdze's house was not as gigantic as it seemed, the rooms were never spacious, but they were in infinite supply. Tzdze's house seemed to have sprouted out of the ground; its rooms were not laid out regularly; the plan (if any) seemed to favor unexpected openings, most of them small, affording unusual vantages onto other parts of the house, including parts that were almost inaccessible. This accounted for the frequency with which I saw Tzdze during the day, even though we never properly encountered each other except in the ways I have already mentioned, never casually or accidentally. I would see Tzdze through small windows set in the walls, often through the triangular trapdoor in floor of the fourth-storey portrait gallery, or from one of the many indoor and outdoor balconies (most of which were small, like theatre boxes), or from the many extremely high spiral staircases, or passing in one of the elevators. Tzdze's house was in this way like a gigantic crystal chandelier, reflecting and multiplying her image. Tzdze was always talking with the servants, issuing new instructions, much of which, from what I could overhear, since the walls and floors were riddled with openings, concerned the preparation of meals, and she was accompanied by Xchte everywhere she went. I would usually come to rest in the fourth-floor portrait gallery. The most important paintings were kept in this gallery, the rest were scattered throughout the house. Most of the walls in Tzdze's house were covered with heavy brass vines, but often a tapestry would be hung over the vines and then portraits would be hung over the tapestries. As a consequence Tzdze's house was not only filled with Tzdze's face and form but with all its antecedents. Tzdze's ancestors' pale faces and hands, and throats and breasts, threw off an extremely faint, chalky, ebbing light that misted the rooms like incense when there was no other light. I felt at home with them. There was no end to them. Any one of them could have stepped from his frame into the room behind my back, slipped out into the forest without being noticed by the servants, who were also everywhere and also resembled the portraits, although this was a resemblance of familiarity, I'm saying this resemblance was acquired through familiarity, and not inborn as was the case with Tzdze.

Now that I say it, it is truer to say that the resemblance began with Tzdze, not with the portraits or the originals. The resemblance is only possible as a connection working backwards from Tzdze, even in the case of her younger sister. There, the resemblance was nevertheless only partial.

When Xchte was present, then more of Tzdze's past, especially her family past, was present, at the margin. Xchte afforded a weak idea of Tzdze's prior life and its source. Otherwise it was impossible not to think of Tzdze as an eternal and uncreated person; I'm exaggerating to avoid the greater error of understatement. I'm feeling stronger and stronger as I write, as my life passes more and more into the writing and out of my body. Soon it will all be worthless to everyone. These portraits have none of the vulgarity and hysteria of mirrors—I think I would be driven insane if I had to stay in a house filled with mirrors, perhaps with even one mirror. Over backgammon, I told Tzdze that I was first shown a mirror in the capital, shortly after I arrived. The reflection I saw made little impression on me, I knew the way I looked and was very satisfied to ignore the way I looked. I wore whatever came to hand and dressed haphazardly until my marriage, when my wife started picking out my clothes. I had never known what to wear or why I should bother thinking about clothes in the first place. Tzdze always dressed in similar clothes, almost always in white with pearls. I don't think that Wite owned a change of clothes. I had always dressed like a down-at-heel clerk, although on the day I met Wite I was wearing my best suit. I had on my best suit only because it happened to come to hand as I got ready to join the Prince's party, and for that matter it was my best suit only because I liked it best for some reason, there was nothing especially impressive about it. I'm still wearing it. I expect I'll be buried in it. I would never have expected it to last this long. I'll never wear anything else, unless they put a shroud on me. I remember, after they brought me here, when they came to take me for my hearing. I had to stand between two men in a cavernous hall, waiting to be admitted into the judge's chamber. There was a huge mirror on the wall opposite the chamber door, and as I was compelled next to sit on a bench along the wall, by the judge's door, with my two guards on either side of me eating sandwiches, I saw myself there every time I looked up. I didn't recognize myself. I looked nothing like the reflection I remembered in the first mirror I had seen in the capital. I had to wait a long time, and I would look down and try to keep my eyes fixed on the spot where the opposite wall met the floor, but every now and then my eyes would turn up to the mirror, and for a few minutes I would have trouble finding myself in it, I blended in perfectly with the furniture and the panelling. The guards were always clearly visible. Then when I did see myself, I would suddenly see myself, that is I would suddenly realize that what I was looking at was me, and I almost screamed. It was a relief to be brought before the judge and sentenced.

I loved Tzdze's patience as she played. Tzdze played more or less slowly but her concentration never drifted. Whenever she asked me about myself or my wife Tzdze seemed to be asking me to help her concentrate, and I'm going to be ruthless and tell you that I was glad to use my past shamelessly like that, to empty it out for Tzdze's concentration. I looked forward to playing with her mostly for this, as a matter of fact. Tzdze asked me about my wife's illnesses and I said that she usually got pains in her legs and shortness of breath, and prolonged dizzy spells. Sometimes her dizzy spells were so severe that she would cling to the edges of the bed and press her face hard into the pillows, and often she would be sobbing. I did everything she asked and I preferred it that way, although she suffered, and to this day I still think of her illnesses with great pain. At worst, she would lie in bed and fuss while I tried to work and look after her as well. My wife was impatient and sickness made her fussy, but I knew that she was still suffering, as she got better she wouldn't know what to do with herself and this feeling in particular would bring her desperation to the surface, she really only knew how to be sick, or it might be better to say that, when she started to feel better, she would get frightened, she would begin to feel that something was expected of her again. These illnesses always interfered with her in a certain way, so that she couldn't simply dispense with them the way other spirit-eaters do. She didn't blank professionally. It occurs to me now I never saw her do it; I think it revolted her. And her illnesses would interfere, even when I tried to help her. When I offered to use my limited skill to help her, she would shrink from me in horror, as though I had offered to do something appalling. What she was expected to do I'm sure I don't know, she certainly didn't know and was frightened, and she would turn desperate. All the people who have ever been around me, except perhaps for my uncle Heckler and Tzdze, have been desperate.

My desperation was already so chastened by then that it could only arise from outside, I was already completely skeptical of it and gave it nothing but practical reasons, and now it gets no reasons from me at all, I've left off with it.

Wite had disappeared entirely, sighted in these days only occasionally, prowling around the foundations of the house, never at the stone outbuilding. Wite seemed to have lost all interest in the stone outbuilding. From what the servants said, Wite was spending most of his time indoors in unused parts of the house, and he seemed to be nearing complete collapse. Tzdze and I were spending more and more time playing backgammon, adding another hour every day until we spent nearly every waking moment playing backgammon, and our rate of play was forever accelerating, the pieces flew off the board under our hands and leapt back again every ten minutes, then every five, then every minute and soon faster still, our hands would weave between each other over the board like schooling fish, and I noticed that Tzdze's hands moved in a regular criss-cross pattern as she played, and as I began to use the same gestures inverted to my side of the board I found I could play as fast as Tzdze did, making every move automatically without thinking, and that this mode of automatic play could completely satisfy the demands of the game while requiring no thought, and as we played under a hypnotic spell over which the hours slid by as only a purely external fact while within us time stood still, while our heads and bodies remained completely motionless and our hands streamed precisely between each other creating in each case a unique game, and during this time I never once looked up at Tzdze's face nor saw any part of Tzdze but her hands flashing between mine over the pieces and the board, and I'm sure that, had I looked up I would have been completely banished from history by the unendurable look of Tzdze's face entranced. Well let me exaggerate, it's better than saying too little. The pieces flew off the board and clattered together on the table to either side in perfect piles. As we played we would sometimes lean forward and then I would feel the crown of her head only a few inches away from mine, and occasionally there would be a sparking across, and a circuit would come briefly into existence from our hands linked across the board by the pieces up our arms and the so on into our heads. We sat across from each other and played all day, faster and faster, and we didn't look at each other even when we came into the room. And during this time Wite was seen only very rarely, in a serious state—this is what one of the servants called it—tenaciously haunting the abandoned parts of the house and its foundations.

One night I woke up to find him sitting at the foot of my bed. His face was pale and blue. He shook. He waited while I dressed and then left the room. I followed him outside. We climbed the bluff behind the house. The slope was covered with tall grass. We reached the top together and Wite stopped in front of the stone outbuilding. The wind was blowing at a constant rate, causing the branches of the trees and the blades of grass to nod back and forth regularly. I could hear one cricket. Wite walked toward the stone outbuilding. I had not yet been up there to see it. It was a small stone pavilion with a round base flush with the ground, eight feet in diameter, ringed with a banister and four columns, and topped with a conical dome. There was a narrow gap in the banister on one side, wide enough to admit one person at a time. Wite stepped under the dome and stopped. He was sweating. Wite placed his hands on the banister, and he was shaking more—more urgently now. His eyes widened and watered.

Wite was looking away from me, across the top of the bluff, into the trees. He had told me he intended to kill himself in there. The outbuilding was made all of grey stone, carved but not polished, deeply pitted and cracked with age, blasted by the weather. Wite stood in the stone outbuilding and shook, looking across the top of the bluff, with his hands trembling on the banister. He was crippled with fear. Wite took me across the bluff, away from the stone outbuilding and into the trees, to a place where there was a shallow depression in the ground behind a low hummock topped with enormous rustling pines. He had stood in the stone outbuilding and had stared in this direction, across the bluff, through the trees, toward the shallow depression and the low hummock. Wite showed me a cave, formed by an overhang of rock held together in the grip of the roots of the trees overhead, making a low arch. The cave floor was an inclined slab of rock that lined the bottom of the shallow depression and climbed up under the arch. The mouth of the cave was diamond-shaped, like an eye. Wite went inside. I couldn't go in. He took my arm and pulled me in a few feet. The cave was not deep. Wite showed me a high shelf at the back of the cave. He pointed it out to me and made me understand that he wanted his body left on that shelf after he died. He was showing me where he wanted me to put his body. I felt I was smothering. He released me and I left the cave.

We walked together to the bottom of the bluff. Wite told me that he was going to kill himself there soon, but that he did not have the strength. He said, "I'm not of one mind about it yet," and saying this he looked exhausted. In fact, he looked so thoroughly drained I find it hard to describe. Wite told me that he would wear himself down into doing it, and then changed his mind and said that he was going to build himself up into doing it. Then Wite told me that he was glad to see me spending time with Tzdze, and that he hoped we were good friends. He told me that he hadn't said anything to her about killing himself. At that time apparently she knew only that he was a fugitive—he said that he owed her a word of warning. It had never occurred to me before that Tzdze was placing herself at risk for harboring him, and that she accepted this risk, as I'm sure Tzdze would have accepted any consequence, without trying to profit, without calling any attention, and without thinking twice. What an idiot I was! This was entirely characteristic of her. Wite asked me if I had told Tzdze that he intended to kill himself there. I said no, and he seemed satisfied. With pain, he told me that Tzdze shouldn't hear of it until he was sure he could do it. Then he added, with his face downcast and in a low voice, that he might need me to tell her.

We were standing outside the walls of the courtyard, a little distance from the gate, and after a while Wite went back into the trees, veering with fantastic speed toward the bluff. Before Wite left me he instructed me to spend my time with Tzdze as I had been and not to seek him out unless the Alaks came. Wite said haggardly that some other thing, beyond everything else, was worrying him. When he left, Wite was picking his legs up straight off the ground and setting them down again like crutches, and he could barely manage to walk in one direction, then his white face shot away in almost a streak into the gloom of the woods. I watched him go and went inside.

Now Tzdze and I were playing less and speaking less. What we had to say to each other worked itself out in empty translation on the board. The secrets I kept for Wite seemed to make me numb toward Tzdze. I began watching her face again as we played, and, for me, Tzdze was now simple and untroubled in such great contrast with her cousin, unconcerned and innocent. Then she told me that we would limit ourselves to one hour of play from then on, and, after we finished, suddenly Tzdze stood up and asked me to come with her. She took me to the uppermost floor of the house, leading me through passages that had been blocked to me before. I followed her through a thick ebony door, whose edges were skirted with thick leather dampers that made a seal against the frame, into what I took to be the largest room in the house. It was filled with large planters of polished brass overflowing with a weird abundance of tropical plants, although the air was quite cold. There were no windows, but the ceiling, which was peaked, and the upper part of the walls, were all thin panels of marble through which there filtered a snowy white glow. It came from every direction, so there were no shadows.

There were convoluted paths traced among the planters, where Tzdze and I walked together. As we walked, Tzdze said only that she spent a great deal of time here. Presently we came to a small fountain flanked by two stone benches, where we sat. I can see that fountain in front of me—a basin shaped like an upright shell and a stone figure leaning against it, her feet in the water: she had her arms crossed and her head was lowered, her eyes stared straight ahead; the water poured down over her in a smooth sheet, although I didn't see how it was conveyed above her head, and it made only the faintest crinkling sound as it returned to the basin. This figure attracted my attention because, while it had been worn thoroughly smooth by the water and its features had been erased, it struck me as the image of Tzdze. I told her so and Tzdze looked at it with a complicated expression on her face. She told me that her relatives had sent a young man to pay suit to her a few days ago, and that he had only just left. I think I said only that I didn't know anything about it or that I hadn't seen him. Tzdze said that her relatives had never accepted her decision—her decision to remain unmarried. For their sake she tolerated these visits, although she received notice only days before her suitors were due, she was given only late notice deliberately, so she wouldn't have time to refuse. These men were forced upon her by her family, but Tzdze didn't seem to mind. I said I thought they were treating her badly. I remember Tzdze flexed her eyebrows at that, and said she wanted them simply to accept her decision to remain unmarried. Then she added that she would gladly receive suitors for her sister. As she said this her eyes were on the ground. Tzdze quickly told me that she was bored and lonely.

I happened to glance away for a moment just as she spoke and I saw Xchte running between a pair of planters some distance away—she had not come with us; she had come some other way. Tzdze did seem bored and alone to me. She asked me what I did with my time, and I said that I generally wandered around the house or read in one of the libraries, that I read a great deal. We talked intermittently for a while about the books we liked, although I never did enjoy reading. When I think back on our conversation, it strikes me that Tzdze and I had both been eluded. I know that in my case there's nothing that cancels life more efficiently than pressing crowds of bodies on all sides. These four walls are about to burst in on me from the pressure of all the bodies piling up against them, and this pressure can only mount and mount. The world is filling up with people and their leavings, and as the one increases so does the other, and the horror and boredom just escalate to infinity until you're throttled by them. My life was throttled out of me right from the start, as was Wite's, as was even Tzdze's. Only here and there a few chinks in the heap are still open and still present a bit of light and room, a small bit of stillness to admit some life, but there is death all around those chinks—to try to find that much space, which is tantamount to getting a glimpse of the horizon once and a while, or to claim any sort of life for yourself, life to live in that is, not life to slave in, that is next to impossible. People treat each other with terrible cruelty in all cases, and people endure cruelty in the hopes that it will be given to them one day to enjoy their own cruelty—it's their faith that one day they will be given license to be cruel that keeps them close in with all the others and gives them strength to go on. The only sensible thing to do is leave.

Tzdze said she was worried about Wite, that she had seen him on the grounds and that he looked so miserably weak. I agreed with her and said nothing else. She was certain, as I was, that the Alaks would come, and she was frightened that Wite would do something terrible—something terrible *to them*. I don't think Tzdze said nothing about herself or about the possibility that Wite would be captured. I was thinking of Wite on the bluff, staring at the stone outbuilding, thinking it over, thinking it over, thinking it over. I was sitting there looking at Tzdze, thinking it over, thinking it over. I never approach women.

That night I dreamt, or fantasized, I was in the greenhouse, or whatever it was, that I had gone there perhaps to look for Tzdze. It was cold and the light from the ceiling and walls was fading, and it was growing steadily more quiet—I was surrounded by towering vines, broad leaves, and gigantic flowers, and then as it grew darker and quieter still, I was alone and stilled in the vaults beneath the house. I could see the tombs of Tzdze's ancestors all around me, where no light was, but I could still make them out. A spirit is obscure even in plain view, but most of my power had lodged in my eyes, I had the keenest sight of any spirit-eater, and I could dimly see them. Their bodies were withered away, but they remained whole and undiminished. I was unable to look at them directly, but sometimes I would turn and inadvertently I would see one so clearly that almost I could feel his breath on my face or even taste the taste of her mouth as if it were mine. They looked remembered. They were all familiar. Each was endued with an old life.

I stood among them and the tombs, which were all covered with carvings of their faces and with dust, and I heard nothing but quiet and spiders. Sometimes it would rain outside and the water might trickle in. Occasionally the door would open for another one, who would enter head first and on the back. I could see thick stone columns and the tombs very faintly from the light that shone under the door. I heard footsteps coming very faintly near. Then they were close, heavy, and uneven. I saw a shadow appear in the strip of light under the door, all but blocking it totally—the door began crashing in its frame as whatever it was on the other side was battering it and I knew that the door would give way and something insanely violent would come bursting through. These same sounds woke me in my room, and part of me was still dreaming, downstairs in the vault, while I ran down the stairs and found the doors there standing open and I followed down the steps to the basement and the sub-basement, and from the inside, in the dream, I felt and saw the door burst open and crash shuddering against the wall with Wite standing in the doorway; he didn't come rushing in, but something of him came gaping in. I saw him standing in the doorway as I came down the stairs, and by the time I reached the floor he had raised his arms, his hands were shaking and I could see his knees were trembling too, and his whole body seemed brittle, painful, and weak to me. Wite lowered his hands. I stopped; I felt the air in front of me grow dense and it pushed me to the floor like a weight; when I looked I could see a very faint streak of light in the air in front of Wite, curling around his two lowered and outstretched hands in the shape of a diamond; I was smothering. I felt a draught from the door that steadily increased as the density of the air grew less and I was being blasted backward so I couldn't stand up, while Wite stood in the door with the tails of his coat flying back and his hands clawed the air, and I was thankful that I couldn't see his face; part of me still dreamed and saw his face, saw that what he was doing was *deliberate*. I remember thinking that he was drawing up into himself the strength to die. The pathetic and withered relics that lay all around me shivered apart and collapsed utterly; the whole vault was pandemonium as they were sucked out, and I had to watch everything. I watched it. Wite pulled them, the spirits of Tzdze's ancestors, out and devoured them one by one, and they were pleading with him and calling him by name while he was doing it, his own ancestors. I could see his cold face as he was doing it.

When Wite lowered his hands I came fully awake as the draught stopped and he turned to me, I powerlessly looking up at him from the floor, he looking back at me coldly, shocked. Wite was well-fed; his hands had stopped shaking and his legs were steady, his back was unstooped and his eyes had cleared from milky grey to green. He very simply walked past me and went vigorously up the steps. I was back on my feet by then, as he was reaching the top of the steps. Even from where I stood I could see that the vault beyond was empty and suddenly immemorial.

CHAPTER SIX

———

I was unsure, I was unsure, I was thinking it over, whether or not to tell Tzdze what Wite had done. I don't want to think about it, I'll confess I wanted to keep it from Tzdze, I had no idea what I wanted. Tzdze and I were spending almost all of our time together. I'd never spent much time together with any one in my life. I didn't want to think about anything else—but of course I had to tell Tzdze in time. Tzdze and I spent all our time together and it was unheard of for me to spend so much time in someone else's company, even my wife's.—At this point as I look back and remember I can only babble about Tzdze. I can't speak responsibly about her. I know I'll have to be more responsible. I get overly filled up with my memories of her.

Tzdze and I stopped playing backgammon altogether very soon after Wite robbed the crypt, because Tzdze wanted to make a portrait of me. She had decided to make a portrait of me entirely on a whim. She had no idea what Wite had done in the crypt. We had been standing in front of a portrait of Xchte, which had been made when she was only four or five years old, one that Tzdze had painted, and Tzdze said all at once that she wanted to make my portrait. I had been loitering in the portrait gallery alone, sitting still and staring at the air in front of me without thinking as always, when I looked up and saw Tzdze, and she glided in and began showing me the paintings. Very vividly I remember a family scene of Tzdze as a child with her parents, and Wite as well. Tzdze was ten when the portrait was made, and inside the frame her image was reclining in the grass at the foot of her mother's divan, lightly grasping a tiny hammer in one hand and a few nails in another, and there was a miniature house standing in front of her on the ground. Tzdze explained that she had loved building things when she was a child, and that she had gone on to build many pieces of furniture in the house, including the backgammon table. But she had given that up, that is building, some time ago. Inside the frame, Wite was standing next to her and nearby in the family portrait, playing good-naturedly with a dog. Tzdze showed me, pointing, that there was candy in his pockets, his pockets were stuffed with candy. We found the painting Tzdze had done herself, a portrait of Xchte when she was four or five years old. Tzdze showed it to me without comment and said she wanted to try painting me. She asked me unhesitatingly, and I agreed to sit for her unhesitatingly. At the time and at present I felt Tzdze had paid me a high compliment by offering to make a portrait of me, although I'm certain she felt she was inconveniencing me by asking. I'm certain she never understood how grateful I was to her for that compliment.

Eventually, Tzdze decided she wanted to paint me in one of the unused lumber-rooms on the ground floor. There were only a few old furnishings put out of the way there, and an angled bench that fit into the corner opposite the fireplace. Tzdze sat me on the bench, by the window, saying "I like the stark light here for you." When the day was overcast, as in that season it always was, the light from the window was stark white. I sat in the corner and Tzdze looked intently at me, and said, "You're most evenly lit when you sit with your arm on the sill." I had lain my arm on the sill when sat down, and she painted me in that posture. She first had one of her servants cut my hair. I was accustomed, in the city, to wear my hair as short as possible, but since I had left it had grown at random. One of the servants cut my hair in my room with the sheep-shears, and then I went downstairs to begin sitting for Tzdze. She had a chair brought in with the easel, and sat sketching me first. After spending a day sketching me, Tzdze and I would meet in the lumber-room each morning and she would paint me as slowly as possible. We never spoke while she painted. I sat as Tzdze instructed me to sit and kept still, and although I began to ache after a while, I was not in an uncomfortable posture. Tzdze painted only very slowly, looking from me to the canvas, from the canvas back to me, at long intervals, without speaking. I didn't speak and was content to remain silent with Tzdze. I was in her presence and I was the object of her complete attention—what did I have to say to Tzdze then? I spent all day sitting with Tzdze and I was content to be silent and motionless in front of her canvas and receive her gaze at intervals. My head was not turned, I was not a foolish old man. Tzdze did not make a fool out of me. If I am a fool, I was a fool before Tzdze met me. Tzdze never treated me like a fool.

I don't know whether she is alive or dead, but I sense her in the earth, in the air, here with me, in this cell, she is here with me now! The sigh that is torn from my breast goes out to meet the chime that chimes from her without wavering—I'm hoping the guards don't come in and disrupt, that they would hear me sobbing out and look in on me, they are always as gentle as possible with me; they are Alaks and have no reason to hate me. Their faces are always full of sympathy when I see them, but sympathy is confined to the breast that bears it and does not come out into the air like Tzdze's ringing arms to hold me, something I never felt in life. Tzdze and I never touched, but I feel her arms around me this moment—my lungs are filling with her breath, which is numbing them, they're expanding and I'm taking the first full breaths I've taken in weeks. Tzdze has given me my life's only freedom. I feel her breath going into my blood, numbing my heart. As I lie in bed at night I seem to see her face as smooth and polished and white as porcelain, looking straight down at me, calmly, exactly as she did when we, Wite and I, appeared beneath her balcony. I simply allow my eyes to open upwards and soon her features become gigantic, spacious, and I can blow across the landscape they make, like dead leaves across perfect surface of the moon, where I am always free to visit the peacefulness. Tzdze is with me and she breathes peacefulness to me.

When I die, beautiful things will sprout peacefully from me and release themselves out of me. I know what's going to happen, where I'm going, and when my dead body blooms, if what blooms from it is beautiful, then it was Tzdze that made them beautiful things. Tzdze prevented Wite from annihilating me. I was not annihilated by Wite, because I knew Tzdze, and for me knowing her was enough. From the moment I met her, my attention was divided between her and Wite, and that preserved me. The part of me that I gave over to Tzdze was a reservation, and was not devoured by Wite as so much else of me was. Even before I knew that I loved Tzdze—imagine my falling in love with her!—that love remained possible for me made it possible for me to love Wite. Where Tzdze remains, I know she has escaped Wite and has nothing to fear from him, because Wite never resisted Tzdze in anything, Wite deferred to Tzdze in everything with only the one exception, and that was possibly intentional, if I assume that Wite fully understood what Tzdze would do. I bear Tzdze with me, wherever Tzdze is I bear her with me now, she wears the white veil of her will. She is my only infinite future world. I intend to go out to meet her soon, as I know I will go out like a light I will go out to see Tzdze, if only to take my final leave of her—and I believe I will see Wite again. Wite is always almost imperceptible. In person, he brought along an interposing distance, and that remains. As he is now, Wite wants us to imagine him like rivers of lava under cool earth, like the sap that rises in the trees. Wite says he is the sap running in the boughs that weave together from tree to tree, which, according to Wite, link every tree in the forest to each other, and that the entire forest has one steady pitch-pulse that he determines, and as the pitch rises in the trunks it somehow forces the roots deeper together, weaving them together also, under the ground, and driving them into the rocks and streams of melted rock. Wite insisted there were streams of melted rock under the forest floor, and said that there were roots of precious stone waving in a white stream of melted rock beneath our feet, which was, according to Wite, identical to the white seam between thunderheads for example or at the horizon for example. These were some of the things Wite actually said to me directly, or attempted to say, but much later, after all this.

I hadn't understood why Wite had gone into the crypt, but this continued to trouble me and I intended to tell Tzdze. From the night that it happened I knew that Tzdze had to be told, but I suspected, I suspected even then that Wite had intended that I tell Tzdze that he had robbed the crypt. We sat together in the lumber-room, and at that time Wite almost never showed himself, Wite was almost never in the house, and Tzdze painted me in silence and I sat for her portrait in silence. I had waited, without realizing it, to tell her. When I looked across to her from where I was sitting, I considered telling her, but it was impossible. Speaking to Tzdze, let alone telling her what had happened in the crypt, was impossible then. I amazed myself when I opened my mouth and told her succinctly that Wite had robbed the crypt. The impossibility of speaking to her was so strong it had become tangible, like a gag in my mouth. My mouth had been completely stopped up, about Wite and about anything else, and then I abruptly opened my mouth and said, "One night last week, I woke up thinking that something was wrong, and I ran blindly downstairs. I found Wite had broken into the crypt in the basement. I saw him eating the ghosts he found there." I could not have told her that I was unable to stop him, and I could not have told her that this was the first moment I had had the strength to tell her.

I did not want to *lower myself* to speak on my own behalf, and that has not changed. I remember that I didn't move as I was speaking with Tzdze, that I slouched and that my mouth fell open and I talked from inside myself, with no physical effort at all. All my energies were directed at the impossibility of speaking, which they overcame to my surprise, I never expected even this much of myself. I was tense and exhausted, and I was anxious, thinking that Wite might somehow be hearing me, but I found no lack of strength to speak, I was decisive, I wasn't drained by speaking, I felt drained after I had spoken but not by speaking, I was drained by the surprise and the confused feelings that followed. I loved Tzdze enough to tell her that Wite had robbed the crypt. I had found unexpected decisiveness in myself. I had no intention of defending myself to Tzdze, I was willing to accept her judgement. Tzdze stopped painting immediately and set her brush down.

I was suddenly too tired to see her face clearly, it had an unreadable expression, and my head was whirling. Without a word Tzdze left the room. Only moments later, I remember feeling as if I had woken up without having first been asleep, and I knew at once that Tzdze had abandoned me, because I was always Wite's accomplice, this was her judgement on me. I found out later Tzdze had closeted herself upstairs with Xchte, and she stayed there for days. I saw nothing of either Tzdze or Wite and was entirely alone in the house, except for the servants. I ate with the servants and spent the rest of my time feeling useless, and desperate whenever I thought of Tzdze feeling betrayed. From the moment she and I first met, I would have sworn in complete sincerity to anyone at any price that I would never betray her, and already I had betrayed Tzdze so that she avoided me entirely and thought of me as no better than her cousin. This is why oaths are worthless—it's possible to swear to anything in complete sincerity and be compelled immediately to break that oath without ever once taking the trouble to be deliberately twofaced. Neither an effort nor an intention to deceive is necessary, even a sincere oath is too brief a gesture to be anything more than a fleeting enthusiasm. Tzdze avoided me in her own house, without asking me to leave or giving any word to me at all. I could only wander through the house and grounds nearly frantic with worry, or is that the word? I worried, certainly, but I don't think I did worry about Tzdze. I only grieved for having offended her, with episodes of great agitation, when the feelings became intolerable. When I missed her. I missed her all the time. Weeks went by and I was continuously ill with worry, and so on, I felt that further decisions were being made about me up above, in the upper part of the house, and without me. I had to imagine Tzdze gazing invisibly down on me and making up her mind about me. I seemed to feel Tzdze's gaze everywhere, so that even a little mistake I might make, something embarrassing, even when I could be certain I was alone, would come to her attention somehow and be counted against me.

Tzdze summoned me and spoke briefly with me. She asked me why Wite had gone into the crypt, and I had to confess that I didn't know. I hadn't spoken with Wite after he had robbed the crypt, nor for days before. I had nothing to add to what I had already told her. Tzdze asked me if Wite had come to the estate to rob the crypt, and, when Tzdze asked that, I knew that Wite had said nothing to her, that he had left *everything* to me. Wite had done nothing since our arrival at the estate, he had only robbed the crypt. Wite had gone again and again to the stone outbuilding and had done nothing there. It occurred to me that he had been waiting for me, however long I might be in doing it, to tell Tzdze why he was there, and if Wite had been forced to rob the crypt to stay alive in the meantime, then I had, by hesitating, or rather, by failing to understand what was expected of me, caused him to do it. Without knowing, I had been the cause of everything, if Wite had only been waiting for me to tell Tzdze why he was there, that he intended to take his life in the stone outbuilding. Tzdze hadn't been told, she knew only that Wite was a criminal, running from the Alaks, and that I was his accomplice. At the time, I had no way of knowing whether or not she understood what Wite was, that is that Wite was not any longer a human being. Tzdze knew only what I had told her about Wite's visit to the crypt, he had devoured the ghosts that were there. While I was telling her, in the lumber-room, what Wite did, Tzdze had said nothing, and I had no way of knowing whether or not she understood how Wite had been able to do what he did—but Tzdze clearly believed me.

I asked Tzdze if she knew that Wite had been a spirit-eater, and that

I was a spirit-eater. She said—yes—impatiently and explained that Wite had already told her, then asked me again if he had come to the estate to rob the crypt. Then, as succinctly as possible, just as before, I said, "No, he came here to kill himself in the stone outbuilding." Tzdze was silent immediately. No, I mean to say that she was taken aback by my words and no longer seemed inclined to converse. I sat without thinking. Some time later, Xchte came into the room and led me to the door by my arm, coming through with me and shutting the door behind us, between us and Tzdze. Xchte brought me to the end of that hallway, where there was a window, and told me quietly that, when Wite had first arrived, Tzdze had told him that she wouldn't shelter him at the estate if he was—Xchte stopped.

She said that Wite had come to see Tzdze alone, and that she, Xchte, had been there, in the room, with them, and that when Wite first appeared and explained what had happened, when he had told Tzdze why he was running from the Alaks, Tzdze had been upset with him, had raised her voice. Xchte quietly said that Wite had begun throwing off a little light, that, when Tzdze spoke harshly to him, he shuddered in the air like the light of a candle—Xchte used those words—and when Tzdze saw what Wite was doing, she had screamed and covered her face. Wite had been forced to leave the room, Tzdze was terrified, she couldn't abide it, the power and the strangeness and the inhumanity and the dreamlikeness of Wite then made her virtually hysterical. Tzdze would become hysterical because Wite's strangeness was *unbearable* to her. Xchte said that Wite was concerned for Tzdze, and that, when she had recovered, Tzdze made Wite promise never to—Xchte stopped. I told her then that I understood, that Wite was not to do what he *could*. Xchte had seen everything, and had chosen to tell me then because she had sympathy for me. Xchte had felt I should know, and spoke to me once only, to tell me that Tzdze had forbidden Wite to do what he *could*, which was unbearable to Tzdze; this meaning of course that Wite had doubly betrayed her in having robbed the crypt as he had. From the window, Xchte had left me there, and I raised my eyes to the glass and I saw Wite at the stone outbuilding. He turned and looked directly at me in the window.

There was no doubt in my mind that I had been abandoned by Tzdze. I had been abandoned by Wite and Tzdze, or I had abandoned Wite and Tzdze, without intending to, there was no talking to them, I stayed there wanting to see them again and no one would speak to me. I didn't know what I would do. The next morning I awoke in a panic, and I heard footsteps rushing in the hall outside my door. The servants were racing through the house, and Tzdze came up to me as I came out onto the landing. I remember Tzdze brought her face directly up to me, and I saw the alarm that was there. She took my arm and said, "The Alaks will be here within the hour. One of my servants had word from the woodcutters, the Alaks are coming quickly with soldiers, for Wite."

Tzdze said, "I've sent two of the porters to bring Wite to the house." Tzdze took hold of my arm and urgently spoke to me, "You will have to take charge of him. He must know nothing about the soldiers—*there's no telling what he is capable of doing*—take him and hide him, I've made a room ready and I'll show you where it is. Keep him there until the Alaks are gone—don't tell him anything." Tzdze showed me the room, all empty and made of stone, a heavy door on powerful hinges, with a stout crossbeam to hold it shut. "Keep him there. Shut him in until the Alaks are well away. Do whatever you can." Tzdze left me. A moment later, two porters brought Wite to me where I stood. Wite had come with them without a word and was docile, his face was grey and yellow, he looked worn out. I hadn't been close to him in days, I had forgotten how deteriorated he was. Wite didn't speak or seem to notice the confusion around him, and the porters handed him gently to me and waited at the head of the stairs. The room Tzdze had prepared was pushed far to the back of the house, on the side opposite the courtyard, where the walls were thickest. There was only one high, narrow window. It resembled the cell where I am writing now, but it was more spacious—there was a fireplace. I led Wite into the room and sat him on the floor without speaking.

For a moment I was at a loss, I stood there emptyheaded, when Wite asked for water. I remember that his voice sounded as if it were torn from his throat. I sent one of the porters for the water, and he in turn only sent one of the servants to fetch it. When I knelt to give it to Wite, I could smell liquor on his breath. Wite stank entirely of liquor. I went to the porters, and they explained that Tzdze had sent them with brandy, that Wite was filled up with brandy on Tzdze's orders, and that he had drunk it readily. Then word came, passed quietly up the stairs to myself and the porters, that the Alaks had already arrived. The porters looked at me, and

I looked back into the room, where Wite sat against the wall, sipping his water. I thought of the door shut and bolted against him, holding him inside, and the idea was grotesque to me. I shut the door and bolted it anyway. I closed the door as gently as I could, as if I was fooling him, as if Wite wouldn't notice.

I played an idiot's game with Wite, pretending he wouldn't notice as I shut him in an empty stone cell, like the one in which I'm writing now, with a thick wooden door, and slid fast a bolt thicker than my arm. But I did it, I sealed Wite into the room when I heard that the Alaks were already there. I sealed Wite in the room and left the porters to play at standing guard, while I headed toward the courtyard. I traveled toward the front of the house, and I could hear the horses and someone accosting the house from outside in a loud voice. There was no direct route to the front of the house from where I was, at the back, and I was forced to go around past the west wing, in a curve, moving in the direction of the courtyard where Wite and I first arrived, the gates of which were now shut fast against the Alaks. I could hear Tzdze calling her answers back to the Alak voice outside, what I took to be the voice of their head man, and I went once or twice to a window, where they were available, but saw nothing of the Alaks. I was still surrounded by scurrying servants, most of them anxious but doing nothing, and I thought all at once that I shouldn't show myself at the courtyard, that I might be recognized as Wite's accomplice. Perhaps it would be better for me to stay with him. I knew that, if I had been there alone, I would have given myself at once over to the Alaks, for Tzdze's sake—it's almost too disgusting to say by itself, I can say anything in hindsight. I was not there alone, I was with Wite, and Wite had chosen to stay, and I couldn't think a single moment ahead in time, except that I stopped moving toward the front of the house and stayed back away from the windows. The sound from outside the house was growing in volume, I heard the shouts of the soldiers, and suddenly I saw, in my own way, that the Alaks had brought a spirit-eater with them, and that he had seen me, and Wite as well, inside, and that the Alaks were going to break into the house, and I turned to run further into the house, in fear, and also to run to Wite, for protection, and in fear.

I heard a terrible smashing sound, like a collapsing wall. Later, the servants told me they had seen the gate of the courtyard burst outwards, showering the soldiers with splintered wood. At the same moment I heard Tzdze scream somewhere behind me—I glanced over my shoulder and saw Tzdze rush past on the floor above a moment later, running in from the terrace that overlooked the courtyard; her face was stricken. I had a nightmare feeling. I ran further into the house, upstairs to a balcony on one of the terraced floors, and by the time I reached the balcony I could hear the soldiers and horses screaming—before I saw or heard them I knew they were being slaughtered from the screaming—when I reached the balcony I could see—the ground was littered with torn bodies, and something was moving among the broken ranks of soldiers, trampling and tearing them apart.

Most had turned and were fleeing toward the woods, their commanding officer was pale, his body streaming with blood, his horse hysterical but reined in, bobbing beneath him and shuddering, very terrified and showing the whites of its eyes visible to me even over that distance. I clearly remember the whites of its eyes and its bared teeth, and the commanding officer was ordering his men in a fainter and fainter voice to take refuge in the house, gesturing with a wavering hand to the shattered gate, the color was leaving his face more and more as the blood sluiced down his sides—he collapsed and fell, his horse trampled him in its panic to escape—I looked away and saw the fleeing soldiers swept from their horses and pulped against the ground, two at a time, as if they were caught in an avalanche—above their screams I could hear a howling voice that came from inside the house and shook the building—the Alak spirit-eater was sitting beside his blindly kicking horse, its blood had spattered him as it fell, and the Alak spirit-eater sat on the ground bolt upright staring with his mouth open—when I looked again—but I couldn't see it, it was too big—a moment later something surged out from a tangle of red bodies and the Alak spirit-eater screamed once, then where he had been there was only a red crater. He was the last—they had all died.

After a moment of silence, a wind blew around the house and down onto the red field. All the bodies began to roll along the ground at once. They rolled faster and faster until they came off the ground and fell sideways into the forest. They all disappeared. After a moment the red ground turned green again, the blood boiled off into a red mist and blew into the forest. Even the stink went, and there was nothing.

I ran back inside to find Wite—I can only say that I had to see him. Wite was where I had left him. The door was ajar, the bolt was in pieces, the porters were fled, and inside I could see a flickering glow dying out, that was gone as I came in. Wite was settling on the floor on his face, as if he had been hanging in the air, his body was stiff and shaking, and then it relaxed and seemed to fall apart. Wite settled on the ground. He had struck his forehead against a flagstone, leaving a white mark with cracks, some pulverized stone in the center. Wite's hands were covered in blood, and as I turned him over onto his back his face slackened, his lips dropped over his teeth, also smeared with red froth. His eyes fluttered once and he seemed to fall to pieces, exhausted, weak, all but dead, worn, blank.

CHAPTER SEVEN

———

I felt no sympathy for the soldiers who had come for Wite as if he were a man, when Wite was not a man, Wite had never been a man or he hadn't been a man for a long time. I felt no sympathy for the soldiers, my "co-religionists." They had no idea that Wite was not a criminal or a refugee, that Wite was not a man, although he had been born and had grown up, lived in a city, had done work. But Wite had never been distracted, he had never left his path, or lost sight of the facts. He stayed "on the mountain." He had used those words himself, "on the mountain." Wite stayed "on the mountain" and from there, that is, from *above*, he had grown so "hot" or so "bright"—again, Wite's words—that none of the nonsense of city life and city people could get near him and not be burned up, this was my impression, that Wite burned by proximity everything superfluous, obstacles included. I pitied the soldiers but I felt no sympathy for them—from my position a little "up the mountain." I never blamed Wite for not wanting to "come down to them." "On the mountain" also means at the brink of death, every encounter would have to end in death for Wite or for the others, or both. Wite could never be brought back from the immediate orbit of death, he had thrown himself into that orbit completely and was inextricable, he was the orbit around death and anyone who charged at him there would simply fall in, they would inevitably die. I don't want my own notion of "the orbit around death" to obscure the one fact most important to keep in sight—that Wite killed everyone who came at him. They didn't simply die, they weren't killed accidentally, as if they had charged a volcano, they were killed deliberately by Wite, and I understood this *very* clearly.

I had with my own eyes seen Wite kill everyone in my hunting party, but when I had seen Wite after he had killed everyone in my hunting party, and when I saw him after he had killed the soldiers who came to Tzdze's house, I felt only the sort of excitement one feels when exciting things are happening, during violent storms, during catastrophes. I felt no special fear and ran to Wite without hesitation. Later, when all excitement was worn away, I felt calm when I thought about Wite, even in the expectation that he might kill me somehow. I saw that Wite was a threat to my life and still felt nothing, no concern. *Only Tzdze* held me and instilled caution into me. *Only Tzdze* kept me from indifference, for her sake, because I feared that Wite might somehow kill her, or ruin her. Tzdze was my diversion from the path, she split me off from him, in part. This was also necessary. After I had met Tzdze, I would never belong completely to Wite again, as I had belonged to him completely from the first moment I saw him.

I had seen Wite devour the spirits of the soldiers. He had known long in advance that they were coming, and had robbed the crypt to be ready for them. This much I realized immediately as it happened. Wite was not so strong after that. He was worn out, lay unconscious for days and recovered slowly, leaning on me. Tzdze did not show herself after that, and kept Xchte with her. Wite had devoured the spirits of the soldiers as they died, he wasn't "starving," but, if I can make myself understood, in killing the soldiers he had thoroughly burned himself, the sort of thorough burning that is never thoroughly healed. I want to say that Wite was not reduced by this, but thoroughly scorched and sensitized, that he was thoroughly changed and concentrated in a smaller volume than before, and something like—he was ruptured by the struggle, and his nerves were flayed. For all this, Wite needed time to recover, and he recovered quickly, though not to the same strength as before. Wite said nothing in particular to me. I knew he had robbed the crypt for strength enough to face the soldiers. Wite still hadn't taken his life, and I began to think Wite was afraid.

I began wondering if he would kill himself, or whether he would simply haunt Tzdze's house until more soldiers came and finally killed him. Wite would not have the strength to fight more soldiers, and more soldiers were certainly coming. I knew, from various signs Wite had inadvertently given me, that he didn't want to be killed by soldiers. He had insisted on killing himself, but he still did nothing. When Wite could walk again, he began wandering the grounds and woods as before, but he seemed to avoid the stone outbuilding. Once, when Wite was crossing the grounds and I was watching him as I often did from a window, I saw him glance up at the stone outbuilding and then turn away and move quickly off into the trees. When I saw the expression on his face as he looked up at the stone outbuilding, it dawned on me that he was *terrified*. Even Wite was afraid of what he might do—Wite was terrified of his own plan. I remember leaving the window and going to sit down, and barely making it to the chair. I was so shocked that I nearly fell. I sat there for hours, shocked. It was shocking to think that Wite was *hesitating*, it had never occurred to me that he would hesitate at anything, I couldn't understand Wite hesitating. How could Wite hesitate? It is characteristic of me that I assumed Wite had made a decision, or changed his mind, and that it only then occurred to me, when I saw Wite from the window, that he might be faltering. I remember a dreamlike feeling that I can't describe, I've had this feeling a number of times and, while it is more or less always in my mind I have no control over this feeling, it will suddenly attack me all at once and I will be terrified, thinking that nothing is real, that even I am not real. My wife was one of the few people I've known to recognize this feeling; she said she had once felt something like this dreamlike feeling, as if she and the world were all suddenly struck through with little gaps—her words—the little gaps where things are, without moving apart or disintegrating, anything so clear as that, hanging separate and apart. I had this feeling when I saw that Wite was terrified of his own plan, and irresolutely hesitating.

I sat in that chair for a while. Then at once, uncharacteristically for me, I was all "assembled" and thinking practically. I thought of the soldiers coming for Wite, who would not be able to fight them, and would consequently most likely be killed by them. Much more important to me, I was thinking of Tzdze and the danger to her, from Wite and from the Alaks, who could arrest her for harboring Wite. I went directly to Tzdze's suite, but she didn't answer her door, Tzdze never answered her door to me. She hadn't left her rooms for over a week. I decided to come back the next day. I was reading in my room that night when Tzdze appeared at my door, wearing a terrible face, and frantic.

Tzdze came directly up to me and seized my arm—she said, "I've poisoned Wite—he's still alive! I gave him strong poison and he drank it all, but he hasn't died!" I don't think I understood. She said, "I put it in his brandy, he drained the bottle and is still alive, downstairs at the table!" Tzdze was shaking my arm and trying to pull me along. She said, "He drank it and started shaking, and fell on the floor, but he's still alive!" I think I was able to talk then, then or soon after, while Tzdze was moving quickly around the room wringing her hands. Tzdze seemed horrified, she was asking what had she done to no one in particular, certainly not to me, what had she done, what was she trying to do, she was frightened by her own resolution and she was afraid it hadn't worked. To have tried and failed to kill Wite, for Tzdze, was the worst possible thing. I told her something—like this, "Wite is a soul-burner, he can resist poisons. He's using his power to burn off the poison." Tzdze complained that she'd given him an enormous dose, enough to kill a dozen men, she'd thought it would be enough even for Wite.

I told her that Wite was far too strong, something like that, through my confusion. Tzdze took my arm again with urgency and said, "Will he recover?" "Of course," I said, "within the hour, if that long." Tzdze was beside herself—"Who knows what he'll do? He'll tear the house apart, and the servants, *Xchte!*" She was in anguish. "We can't let him!" she was saying, "He must'nt recover, he has to be finished, I have to finish him, while he's still poisoned! Tell me what to do!" I said, with a confidence that puzzles me now, "He will only be able to die in the stone outbuilding." Tzdze implored me to help her bring Wite to the stone outbuilding. She and I went downstairs, to Wite. He was lying on his face beside the table, trying to drag himself forward on his elbow. He was shuddering and had vomited a little. I took him by the shoulders and dragged him to his feet. I could feel Wite burning off the poison, his whole body was buzzing like a plucked wire. The air around him trembled as if with intense heat, and a biting vapor was steaming from his skin. I looked at his face, I saw nothing there. Wite was taller than me and struggling feebly.

I threw my arms around his chest from the front and lifted him that way, telling Tzdze to take his arms and hold them behind his back. Tzdze took his arms immediately, and I carried him outside. Wite was surging up almost out of my arms, but he was weak and delirious from the poison. His head rolled back and forth and he gave a few little screams. Wite's body was light and brittle-feeling, but I felt it pounding against me, as if it were bursting at the seams, and jerking upward nearly out of my grip. Tzdze was looking at me with her eyes nearly screwed shut, her whole face was screwed shut and closed, shut down on itself. I realize this describes nothing clearly but I have no right to put Tzdze's distress too plainly before you. We carried Wite swiftly up the slope to the stone outbuilding. He was scarcely any weight at all, even I could carry him and not be tired. I brought Wite into the stone outbuilding and pushed him up against a pillar. Tzdze came around behind and held his hands to either side of the pillar. When I saw Wite, nearly fainting there, held up by my hand in the shadow of the stone outbuilding, against the pillar, with Tzdze's white, stricken face peering at me over his shoulder, I felt a dying feeling as if I was turning to stone. All my intention was gone. Tzdze was—I won't say. She suddenly held up a knife she had brought with her, Tzdze had taken it from the table without my noticing. Tzdze told me to take it, and I found it in my hand. Tzdze was holding Wite's arms. Wite's head was still lolling on his neck, he was fighting to hold it up. Tzdze shouted, "Please!" Wite saw the knife and he began struggling more urgently, muttering, trying to talk to me. I stood there with the knife. Tzdze shouted, "Please hurry!" She was in pain. I stood, holding Wite up against the pillar with my left hand and with the knife in my right, and as I remember I see my hand thrust out in front of me, pressing Wite's rocking chest, Wite was sobbing, his head was upright and shaking a little, looking at me, he said "I don't want to die," Wite told me he didn't want to die, Tzdze was there over his shoulder, saying "Please" to me. Wite was regathering his strength and was nearly fit to defend himself, he was still vulnerable then. My hand only went forward with almost no strength behind it as if I were only giving Wite the knife and it slid in beneath my left hand only a little, Wite almost screamed but his throat was already flooded, the throb of his body was delivered to me across the palm of my left hand and through the handle of the knife, I pushed the knife into his chest to its full length meeting almost no resistance, and Wite was sobbing with a knife in his chest, the sobs being delivered across the palm of my left hand that held Wite up against the pillar and the palm of my right hand that still held the handle of the knife. I felt Wite's dying sobs in my own body. I moved back and Wite collapsed at the foot of the pillar, his arms slipping out of Tzdze's grasp. Tzdze had gone completely silent when I stabbed Wite. I had no blood on my hands. Wite's blood was too congealed. My hands were white. Tzdze came around to fetch me, to try to bring me down to the house. Wite died quickly, as we were rushing away. I had lied to Tzdze when I told her Wite could die only in the stone outbuilding. Where did I find the presence of mind to lie? I wanted to bring Wite to the stone outbuilding, because Wite had said he wanted to die there. Wite had begged me not to kill him.

I killed Wite. Tzdze came and led me back to the house. Wite was still lying at the base of the column with his head at an angle. The head hadn't fallen either forward or backward but had given way to the side and was drooping onto one shoulder, eyes half-open. Wite had said "I don't want to die" to me before I killed him. The knife stabbed him meeting no resistance. Wite's blood was congealed and didn't spill onto my hands, nor was there much on his shirt. Tzdze had let him go the same moment I did. He had collapsed. Wite was already dead when he collapsed at the foot of the column, because I had stabbed him. The knife had gone directly into his heart. It had nicked his heart, because I hesitated. I had felt his heart beat at the end of the knife, through the handle, in my hand, and I stabbed the knife in to its full length. Wite was unable to protect himself. When I pulled the knife out my hands were completely white. I remember watching my white hand pull back the knife. The blade of the knife was only half dark, the other half still shone. Tzdze had made me throw the knife down on the floor of the stone outbuilding, near Wite's foot, which was thrust out in front of him. Tzdze took me by the arm and led me to the house. The next morning I went back to the stone outbuilding.

I saw Wite's body in daylight, and the knife. I picked Wite up and carried him from the stone outbuilding to the cave he had shown me. I put Wite in the cave, on the shelf he had shown me. When I had set him down, the face was turned toward me. I wanted to turn the face away from me, but I refused to reach up and turn the head. I decided to leave the head as it had turned, facing me. There was no decision, I simply couldn't turn his head away from me. I couldn't see the eyes through the glasses. I left the head facing me. Touching his head or his face would have been like a disfigurement. Then I had to go back to the stone outbuilding for the knife. It had not left a stain on the pavings. There were no marks of Wite's blood anywhere in the stone outbuilding. Once I had picked up the knife, there was no sign. I picked up the knife by its handle and carried it to the cave. I had to throw myself forward on my feet to carry the knife to the cave, I had to carry the knife with Wite's blood on it, only just a little of Wite's blood on it, to the cave where the body was lying with its face turned toward the cave mouth where I would come in. I picked up the knife and decided to carry it to the cave and leave it there. I took the knife that I had used to kill Wite to the cave where Wite's body was lying on a high shelf, at the back of the cave in the dark, with its head turned toward the mouth of the cave where I would come in, carrying the knife. I could see the glasses shining when I came in. I went up to his body and placed the knife beside Wite on the shelf, nowhere in particular but beside Wite. I left the knife there and turned my back, and walked out of the cave. I walked down the slope to the house without a look behind me. I just walked down the slope without a glance at the stone outbuilding or back at the cave, or at the trees around me, at anything but the grass and my feet as I walked, and thought of nothing but where to put my feet.

I would not be able to write. It would be grotesque for me to say the slightest thing about any of this, if I weren't called to testify to everything, if Wite hadn't allowed it directly from the beginning. From the beginning he had consciously decided that I would testify to everything, without himself knowing what that testament would be, that much he'll never know, but I was trusted to testify to everything, by Wite. My call was to speak it thoroughly, to the last moment, in every detail as it was for me, and when I finish my lungs will finally fail and I will give myself up once and for all, but my lungs will hold me until I finish. I'm not finished. The stone outbuilding the cave Wite's head turned toward me, the knife that I killed him. Tzdze in the house at the foot of the bluff. Tzdze had poisoned Wite's brandy, as strong a poison as she could find. Tzdze had brewed it as strong as possible. But I stabbed him, while Tzdze held the arms. Tzdze and I both let him go at the same time, to fall down at the base of the column. Wite died and Tzdze and I lived. I don't know whether Tzdze lives, but I still live, and will live until this is finished. When the testament is finished, I will die. And I'm racing along as fast as I can, not because I'm eager to die, but because, whether I die or not, I have to finish my testament for Wite. I write as fast as I can to satisfy Wite, to make this a present for him. I write hastily to give this to Wite all the sooner, death or no death. But I won't die until I've made this in full, a present to Wite, Wite through the world. This is for Wite.

CHAPTER EIGHT

———

I will draw and draw and draw and draw. Years later Tzdze called me back. Tzdze sent word to me to come. I had heard next to nothing from Tzdze and then she sent me word, at last enough time had passed for that. When I saw that Tzdze had sent word to me, when I saw her name on the letter, I was shocked awake. I had been sleepwalking all the intervening time. The exhaustion and outrage and disgust of going on had come down on me so heavily, I thought about nothing all the time, or tried to, I couldn't have any more life than a ghost after I killed Wite. Every thought that entered my head I resented, once I'd left Tzdze's estate. From the start, I knew that I would never outlive that, or emerge from that, I was only lying and wasting time trying to wait myself out in town, of course I lived in town, I couldn't be bothered to look after myself, I went to a town with Tzdze's signet in my hand. When Tzdze heard I was leaving, she sent a porter with her signet to me, the signet—*so that I could find work.* I brought Tzdze's signet with me and took it to so and so and so and so, and I was given this and that to do, money to surrender for a room and food and on and on, in complete bankruptcy.

I took Tzdze's signet from the porter knowing that I was going to use it, disgusted, knowing that I could expect nothing better from myself. After everything that had happened, what else would I do but take Tzdze's signet and drag myself off to *find work?* By that time, I was too indifferent to do anything but the most obvious thing, the most pedestrian, I mean whatever came to hand. Town rose up around me like so much nonsense and the years I lived there made no impression on my memory, they recall nothing, nothing but dullness and sloveliness and tedium, night after night of insomnia, night after night of sloven and raucous noise in the street, my window was right on the street of course, of course my bed was directly under the window, naturally there was nowhere else to put it. Why didn't I sleep in a ditch? Why didn't I sleep with my head down an outhouse? The whole town, it seemed to me, was a huge rubbish heap in which disagreeable people burrowed and fretted. What was its name? It lived only for itself, and only the way carrion lives, or perhaps that's how it seemed to me at the time because that's how I lived then, meeting every dawn, after a loud night without sleep, do I have to go on? Do I have to haul myself up and down the street asking whether or not I am already dead? And with no memory I look back and know with certainty that I worked, that I did some task or other responsibly and was paid, that I was a success at whatever I did, which would have astonished me at the time, if I'd cared, that they didn't want to see me go when Tzdze wrote to summon me. There was no question I would go when Tzdze wrote. Apart from death, Tzdze was the only delivery I had waiting. I went, knowing in advance that the house would be the same, and my eye would be continuously hooked and shocked by the stone outhouse on the bluff, and that I would stand glued to the window, bewitched by the stone outbuilding I had never left. I'm still there at the stone outbuilding, with the knife pushing into Wite, just starting to push.

I went without hesitation, as innocent of thought as any rock sliding down a hill. That penitentiary town put me in a brainless trance, so that even as I was getting ready to leave I had to sleepwalk through the day in a trance—if it weren't for those brainless trances, I would have gone hysterical, they would have locked me away as they've locked me away now, or worse. No they would have left me to rave by the side of the street, and roll to and fro in their muck, and claw at myself until I grew too tired to move. They would have robbed me, of course, and molested me at their pleasure, but they almost certainly wouldn't have locked me up. There were no Alaks or Alak representatives in residence whose face would need saving. I didn't try to preserve myself by being numb and stupid, it came naturally and it made things immensely easier. It didn't wear off until I was well out of town, until I was well clear of those walls, and the horizon had suppressed all trace of them completely. The cobwebs cleared out when I finally managed, I finally got myself in the trees. Nothing clears my mind like trees. I could go on at length.

How will I tell, I draw and draw and draw and draw, how will I tell this? These events have no order in my memory, it is all one event with no end of attached moments, it's all one moment with forever more ramifications. I can only stare back at this time and see-saw from being exhausted to being panic-stricken, just shaking and aggravated to a sort of threshold where I am always nearly dying. I pointed myself at Tzdze's house and set off, but when I found myself on the road in the woods, the narrow road, I woke up all at once and found myself there, as if I had walked there in my sleep, found myself brought along this road back toward Tzdze's house, and it was suddenly like a nightmare, I was being returned to where I had been terrible, to the *very spot*, the house and the stone outbuilding that hovered over it, and the bluff, and the cave where I had put Wite, with Wite over everything, looming over the house and the forest from the heights of the bluff like a headstone, and that's where I was going, to where he would be looking down on me forever. I remember when the trees came apart and Tzdze's house was all of a sudden in front of me.

The courtyard gates were repaired, that was different, and they opened wide for me, and though I kept my eyes down the stone outbuilding was right there, I couldn't help but see it. I saw it and I seemed to feel it sitting on my chest, the spot where Wite had been killed by me shut down on my chest, I saw it and the house beneath it and I felt suffocated just like before. Tzdze's house was opening for me like my coffin, I had come there to step down into my grave and let it close over me, and I felt that start to happen as I laid eyes on the house and the stone outbuilding overhead, and I went ahead even though the air in my lungs was going stale, and my lungs were squeezed shut and tightening. The courtyard gates opened wide for me and I went inside. Tzdze was standing at the balcony. When I saw her, I went all to ice. Tzdze was standing at the balcony, looking down at me like the stone outbuilding, coldly looking down at me, but with no feeling, only as paralyzed and unchanged and blank as me, looking up at her. We reflected each other precisely. We had neither of us budged from the moment of Wite's death. We did not greet each other. I came inside and went directly to my room, which was as I had left it, and was right away just as at home as I had been. When Tzdze and I met face to face, need I say that we had both been counting on our time apart, or just on time, to give us something new, start each of us, or at least one of us, but neither of us had started.

We sat without speaking, in step with each other, certainly, the two most immutable people in the world, the most unreal people, and the stone outbuilding was there at the table with us, walking along behind us, blankly staring back at us as the third party that was she and I together. Don't roll your eyes! Don't think I don't know how I sound—read this however it pleases you to read it. I take it back—roll your eyes all you want, why shouldn't you? I didn't ask why Tzdze had sent for me to come at once, perhaps in the hope that time and new business would have given me something new, and that from my new start Tzdze could start as well, even if she were actually to get up and take only a step away. What was left of the two of us, what wasn't stifled and slowly expiring, was only the exhaustion and panic of being trapped with only your own disintegrating body. We had been reduced to degenerating bodies together, that means we were both only our own deaths, or already ghosts, more ghosts than Wite ever was. I'm not being extravagant—in short, as I'm trying to say, we had something to finish before we could have even an opportunity to go on. One dies, and that's an end, but one outlives oneself and keeps on living an afterlife, and that's unbearable. As ghosts, Tzdze and I were dead without rest, we were able to feel that we were dead, we were dead but things weren't over, and everything we did was shameful and disgusting, horrible, because even just going on without doing anything profaned death for us.

But when I arrived at Tzdze's house, when I saw the stone outbuilding and received from it that shock, as time passed both Tzdze and I began to feel a growing fear, every day greater and greater fear. Without saying anything to each other at first, we could see that we were both getting more and more afraid. I would all of a sudden see that my hands were shaking, and sometimes I saw even Tzdze suddenly seize her hands, to stop them from shaking. We owed it to this fear that we began to change at last. She was afraid of something, so was I, and this fear eventually woke us out of our trance and suddenly we were able to talk to each other, just like that. We started by telling each other that we were both so frightened, and by something new, nothing from that old time. This fear was the new thing that finally happened, only because we were together in that spot. The stone outbuilding was beginning to fade out of our minds because it was being overshadowed by something else more terrible, and we ended up welcoming that feeling, although we were both so agitated all the time, and for no reason, we were jumpy and strained, neither of us could sleep, drinking made it worse for me. I began to think about the stone outbuilding as a respite from this other preoccupation. The spirits had all deserted the house when Wite first arrived, and when he robbed the crypt, but they had not quit the woods, I could see them rushing through the trees like Wite had when I first saw him, with the hunting-party, they were racing everywhere in the trees. I would watch them and nearly collapse from fear, from watching them, where they had never in my life frightened me before. I had eaten spirits, and now they frightened me. What were they now? They had changed, and their behavior was unrecognizeable. I would have lost my mind even seeing one of them up close, but I couldn't stop peering out at them from the window.

I nearly never set foot outside. Tzdze asked me to fetch one of the porters for her, and he was outside. I knew that Tzdze didn't need me to fetch the porter, but I went and looked for him anyway. As I drew up to the trees, I suddenly saw the spirits inside, in the shade, and I wanted to turn and run, but something rushed up and took me from behind and I began walking into the forest. My feet turned *toward the bluff*, I was walking directly up the side of the slope, the path that we always took, the path I carried Wite along to the stone outbuilding, the path I took when I put Wite in the cave. I was walking directly up that path so fast I became dizzy, I looked this way and that and I saw nothing but trees and spirits. Then I saw only trees, and the path through the stones, up the side of the bluff, and then the stone outbuilding was there in front of me, all covered over with moss. I was still walking without stopping, like a condemned man, I was being *pulled along*, and when I took my eyes off my feet that were moving without my intention, against my greatest efforts to move them, I was on the mountain, with the stone outbuilding, I had no way of knowing what I would do next, I had no idea from one moment to the next what I was doing, I couldn't have told you what I would find myself doing in the next minute, the mountain was looming up over me, the mountain was going to swallow me, it was inevitable, I walked on it like a condemned man on the gallows—I took my eyes off my feet and looked up—the cave was in front of me—I was standing in front of the cave mouth and I went right up to it, to the mouth of the cave, I was shaking and I fell, on my knees, my eyes were riveted on the ground in front of me, and then gradually my gaze began to slide forward along the ground, to the shadow thrown down by the lip of the cave, and then I saw inside the cave—I looked up all at once and I saw the two pale spots reflected in Wite's glasses not turned toward me from the back of the cave not turned toward me from the back of the cave not in the back of the cave but from the cave inside the shadows Wite's glasses were reflecting I could see a dim outline there was a dim outline in the cave of Wite I could see that Wite was *standing* just inside the shadow thrown by the upper lip of the cave. He stood there without moving and completely dark against the dark inside the cave but a visible separate mass standing inside the cave, the only light was the light that was reflected from his glasses, the two little spots watching for me and that saw me.

Wite said *hello*. Wite said *thank you*. Wite said *thank Tzdze for me*. Wite said *this mountain is my body now*. Wite said *you're going to tell them about me*. Wite said *tell them to keep off*. Wite said *tell them about ME, Nophtha*. Wite said *take my hand*. I raised my arm and put my hand into the cave. Wite *took my hand*. Wite let my hand go. Wite said *I'll speak with you again*. Wite said *go tell them who the mountain is now Nophtha*. I turned without getting up. I knew I would do exactly what Wite said to do. I knew what he wanted and I knew I would do it, I wanted to. I turned without getting up, smiling, the strangest smile any human being ever smiled, a smile meant for no human person, because I knew I would do exactly what Wite wanted me to do.

I wore that smile as I walked directly down the mountain, it is a horrible smile, meant for no human person and with no human cause, with no moment of its own. It was an inhuman smile, a smile that lasted forever, like the smile of a dead body, smiling for a dead laugh at all life. It is still on my lips.

CHAPTER NINE

———

Did you imagine me coming down the mountain? Did you see it happen, have I written what could be called "a good account?" What did you see? You didn't see me here, in the corner, where I was shaking, where I was terrified and shaking, frozen stiff terrified, grinning. Have you ever grinned in terror? Showing all your teeth? Have you ever grinned for nothing human, not for yourself or anyone, but nothing human and for no human reason? Did you imagine me coming down the mountain? Don't try—who else has ever been haunted by the *gratitude* of the one he betrayed and killed? I went down the slope and I was all turned to weightless glass, I want to say I was coming all apart in sections hanging in the air together. Wite was there behind me all the while, almost as if he walked down with me but he wasn't walking, or moving at all, he was everywhere with me and always concentrated directly behind me, I stopped four or five times and listened, I heard him, back in the cave. He filled up the entire mountain without ever leaving the cave. I would stop and listen, and I would hear him, back in the cave, a high, thin, mindful, quiet, insisting sound that was like a peering over my shoulder, but why would I have run from that sound? Would running have taken it away? I felt my feet place themselves over the ground like glasses, I distracted myself thinking about water glasses being set down, and sometimes turned and almost brought my eyes up to the cave, the stone outbuilding—a high, thin, mindful, quiet, insisting *sound* back in the cave—I distracted myself, I saw that I was floating down the side of the mountain, my whole body was light, thoroughly light, much as it is when I go without sleep, and I lie here exhausted, as light on the side of the mountain as if I'd never slept. I turned my head left and right—I saw no spirits.

Wite had drawn off and devoured them all. There wasn't any sound but a high, thin, mindful, quiet insisting sound, back in the cave. The still air was empty. But did I tell you that my feet were silent? I looked down and my feet were completely silent, I myself made no sound, I was terrified, I was completely silent, like a nightmare, I'd had nightmares and dreamt I couldn't move, perhaps something was coming for me, but immediately I couldn't move, and on the mountainside I could move and was going down the mountain but I was completely silent. I was silent. I was terrified, and grinning. Streaming with tears, grinning, terrified. And then I was thankful for being silent because if I started laughing then and I had heard myself laugh, I would have crossed into insanity. I was not insane. I've never been insane. But there I felt insanity come near to me, so that, if I'd laughed and heard myself laughing then, I would have crossed at that moment exactly into insanity. I was moving steadily, I was silent, I was weightless, and I was completely tensed—that was ridiculous. If you can imagine hiding your head under the covers and counting or holding your breath—I was tensed, I was trying ridiculously to stop myself from—

—and here I can't say from *what*, I could know *that* only if it had happened, and it didn't, because the slope came to an end almost at a right angle to the ground, so that it was possible to say with precision where the mountain rose up out of the ground, and I was stepping down off the slope on the level ground, and the moment I stepped both feet down onto level ground, the spell was stopped. I heard both feet come down onto level ground, and after that I could hear the wind in the trees, which is a rushing sound that is hard to notice without listening for it, and the more obvious sounds, the birds and so on. I heard my breath panting out of me. I remember I sounded like a rusty squeeze-box. I was breathing so hard I nearly fell over on my face. I was immediately distracted and comforted by having such a tired body. I wanted to take note of this in particular, this moment when I crossed over from the slope of the mountain to level ground, and what that was like. This you will follow easily. But I still turned my head once, over my shoulder, and for a moment I heard—high thin mindful quiet insisting—I saw the stone outbuilding, and this time the tension seized me so forcefully I did fall on the ground and rolled over to look at Tzdze's house, turn my full attention on Tzdze's house and the solid level ground on which I rested, which thankfully held me there.

Did you see that—was it clear to you? Let me tell you, that when I first was brought here I had a nightmare, I screamed and was running in every part of the cell, and beating the walls with my fists, I screamed and flailed at the wall with my head tilted back. I know all this because the guards came in and quieted me. They have never lied to me, they wouldn't lie, they would be bad liars if they tried, and I know they weren't lying when they told me I had screamed and flailed at the wall with my head tilted back. One of the guards showed me with little gestures what it was like, without screaming, he lightly flailed a little at the wall and tilted his head back, and they said they were frightened of me, that I was only a silhouette in the cell and that I was screaming and flailing my arms like an animal. I never remembered—not the dream, nor screaming, nor jumping around the room, flailing my arms, nor being taken up and quieted by the guards.

I never remembered. It might never have happened. I know it did only because I trust these guards, who are simply honest Alaks. I know I screamed and flailed against the wall like an animal, that, if one was willing to put it like this, the nightmare had turned me into an animal, and I don't remember it. I have to imagine it just like you do, without firsthand knowledge, but unlike you I know that it was me there. I imagine this horrible scene, with a screaming beastial man in the middle, just as you would, but I have to know that the screaming beastial man was me. Of course, *I'm not Wite*, I'm no danger to anyone. I'm no danger to anyone who doesn't listen to me. I only clear the way for Wite, who is free to do as he likes already. I'm only the instrument Wite uses, as he may freely, as I knew from the first moment I would be. From the first moment I knew I would have to be. Thankfully this does not absolve me. I think I am finally beyond absolving. I'm grateful to Wite to be finally beyond absolving. Wite uses me at will, for what errands he thinks I might be capable of doing, and so I am an extension of Wite. I am bringing Wite to you, as Wite instructed, and his story is my proof that I am part of him and not part of *you*. Not any more, in the past less and less, now almost not at all, soon not at all. When I was young and most like you, what did you do? Like everyone else I was entrusted to the lot of you, like everyone else I found out what that trust was worth—but I was singled out; when I found out what this life was about I wanted only to withdraw, and for that I was specially punished. Does a boy, frightened and hysterical and cringing in a corner, suddenly pull a knife out of his shirt and stab himself?

Don't ask me again why I never took my own life. If you want to know why I hadn't taken my own life, imagine *that*. When I was young, I spent every moment I had to myself up in the hills and in among the trees, alone, where I felt most at ease. I was frightened but much more at ease in the hills, with the trees, than I felt at the house, with my hopeless family. I came in whenever I wanted to and was punished for it. I spent all my own time with the trees. My brothers and sisters spent their time with each other, with their friends, down in the streets, but I spent all my time alone, up in the trees. I was always up in the trees, and I would have lived there as thoughtlessly as an animal if I had been given the choice. I think, looking back, that I would have lived in the trees like an animal, and I know that my memory is confused. I didn't have a clear idea of anything when I was a boy. Now I'm imagining what sense my memories of that time can make. I remember that I was going to change, if I could, into an animal, and that everything in the way the world appeared to me would change forever. I would forget everything. I would correct the mistake and be an animal instead, alone in a new world with no thoughts in my head, without knowing even that my new world was once my old world. Now my head is swimming. I wanted the new world. My head is swimming, I'm completely confused. I remember coming back across level ground to Tzdze's house, and going into Tzdze's house, wanting to see Tzdze. I wanted to see Tzdze in a new world. I waited to see that she was free, I was wondering, I was afraid for her. She had brought me to the house for Wite, without knowing it. I knew he had used her to bring me to the house, Wite loomed over the two of us and was the horizon for both of us. Sometimes it is so easy to write.

I saw Tzdze right away when I came in. Wite was through with her, he had released her at the earliest time, the moment I set out or soon after I had set out to come back, for this visit. Without hearing from Wite, I understood everything like this all at once, intuitively. I would stay in the house and wait. Wite was going to tell me again, after some time, after making me wait. In some ways, Wite rose above nothing, he wasn't above toying a little with me. There's no end to the adjustments I can make in hindsight, and no value to them. I have little to say, but I'll say it over and over to keep it in view, if only to keep my attention fixed. Will you follow my every word, or will you skip a few here and there, and more and more often? I've always been distracted—I hardly know what people mean when they tell me how bored they are, I can barely understand what is this boredom of theirs, a boredom I never feel, I've never been all that bored because I am either not paying attention or paying complete attention.

I sit still and my mind always races. When I lie down to sleep my mind runs off until it exhausts itself, it runs itself to sleep, into the ground. My mind is always running and I am always distracted, so I neglect everything, I never do anything with my complete attention. I didn't neglect Wite. He had my complete attention. I didn't neglect Tzdze. She had my complete attention. I never neglected either of them, and they never failed to command my complete attention. My mind never stopped running but I never neglected them, or failed to give them my complete attention. Wite and Tzdze turned into the terrain that my mind was running through, and that hasn't changed. Now I can barely keep my head up, I can barely raise it over the page, and sometimes I don't bother, I let my head lie to one side and my hand, which already knows these pages, goes on by itself, and the lines do not stray or scribble over each other, the words are all still distinct. But I want to watch my hand write, because, when my head is lying to one side, and I'm not seeing the words, then I see past the edges of my memory. I know I will be there soon. I know I will be past all memory soon. I can barely keep my head up, but my mind races faster than ever, faster than it ever did before, but without tearing everything to pieces, through terrain that is all Wite and Tzdze. When I die, I will go to ground in terrain that is all Wite and Tzdze. I'll have only Wite and Tzdze, entirely surrounding me. When I look past my memories I am looking for Wite, and for Tzdze, and that is my only present temptation. I get paralyzed looking for them there, this is the only thing that stops my hand writing. When I remember Wite and Tzdze, I want to do justice to them, and so I don't let go, I redirect my eyes, so to speak, and set them on the paper again. Who is reading me? I won't ask that seriously yet. I prefer this way, not knowing what I'm doing, not giving shape to things or refusing to.

When I came in, I saw Tzdze right away. She was teaching Xchte, and didn't notice me. She looked fresh. I'd never seen her looking as fresh. If she had seen my face then, she might have seen everything there, but she was distracted with Xchte and I was able to take my face away. I didn't want to imagine what *my news* would do to Tzdze. I had been told to *thank* her. The moment I came in and saw her, I was certain I wouldn't thank her. Then it occurred to me that Wite might decide to thank her personally, and I had second thoughts. I avoided her and waited, because I couldn't make a decision. And then all at once I told her. I told her too abruptly—one moment it was not in my mind to do it, the next moment it was decided that I would tell her at once. I brought her onto the balcony because I had decided, all at once, that I would tell her only there, on the balcony overlooking the courtyard, where I had first seen her. Although we were barely speaking to each other, still hardly able to speak normally, in an everyday fashion, with each other, I was able to bring Tzdze out with me onto the balcony. Together, we were only standing and listening on the balcony. The woods were quiet, I remember they were humid. I had no idea what it would do to Tzdze. I was with her, with my news, and all at once I told her, exactly as I had told her about the crypt when Wite had robbed it. I told her and when I looked I saw the lights reflected in Wite's glasses everywhere in between the trees, and in the fold in the mountain where the cave was, in all the dark that was there, I could see the reflections and Tzdze saw them—all the color left her face. Tzdze shrank back somehow, not quickly, dwindled and shrank back. When I looked again, Wite's glasses were gone. Tzdze was barely visible. I told her that Wite said "thank you."

Tzdze swayed once. I could hardly see her, though she still gleamed in the dark. Her fresh face was gone. I left Tzdze there. I saw her only once more, when I was leaving. I mean in my entire life I saw Tzdze only one more time after delivering Wite's "thank you" on the balcony. The servants were repainting rooms downstairs, the downstairs was full of servants and paint. Tzdze was sitting in one of the rooms off the hall, in supervision, watching some of her servants whitewashing the walls, I suppose. Tzdze was sitting in the middle of the room, not expecting me to pass by, and when I did as I went to leave, Tzdze only glared out the door at me from where she sat. I stood in the doorway, Tzdze sat and glared at me. She did not move, she seemed outraged, as though she were furious; Tzdze glared at me and I stopped in the doorway and for a moment I couldn't move. Tzdze turned her eyes away then, without changing her expression—she didn't see me anymore. Tzdze looked away; I couldn't move. Then I went into the room anyway and stumbled over the doorjam as I came in, I fell a little from the doorway into the room and ended up on my knees by Tzdze's chair. I called to Tzdze without getting up, I touched her hand, a statue's hand, and Tzdze didn't see me any more than a statue would have seen me, kneeling at her feet. Even at her feet Tzdze ignored me, like I wasn't there, although her face hadn't changed. While I was kneeling there I started crying, and while I was crying Tzdze never moved and her face stayed frozen the way it was. She glared at the wall where the servants were still doing their painting. I begged Tzdze to look at me and cried, I forget how I left the room but I know she was always sitting fixed in her chair with her eyes turned away, even when I turned I could feel across my back that Tzdze hadn't moved—she never spoke, I never knew what Tzdze was thinking. I stood in the hall and Tzdze had glared at me, I tried to see inside her glare in my memory, for nothing, I stood there and my good sense had told me to leave right away. I don't trust my hateful good sense. I forced myself to go to Tzdze regardless of my good sense. I had already decided to leave right away but I didn't want to stop trying yet, I had to leave on Wite's instructions but I wanted to stay and stand or kneel in front of Tzdze until she did something, but Wite had wanted me to leave right away. I didn't want to leave. If I never saw Tzdze again—how could I have left her like that? *I* didn't have a choice. I left and I never saw Tzdze again. I never knew anything more about her or what she was thinking about me, except that Wite never molested her.

Tzdze must forgive me. I know that it's impossible for Tzdze to hate me. Do you understand that I must believe Tzdze will forgive me sooner or later, and that Tzdze can't hate me, it must be impossible or else I'm already dead, the fact that I'm still alive is my guarantee: as long as I live, I work, as long as I work I will earn Tzdze's forgiveness even if I have to chase after her soul forever from the moment I die until doomsday, I'll do whatever I have to do and pay absolutely any price until she forgives me. Tzdze will forgive me and must forgive me, and Tzdze can't hate me. This is where this ends.

My uncle Heckler tortured me as part of my apostate education. He tortured me with the eyedrops to inoculate me against torture. The preparation for torture is to be lovingly tortured by your teachers, full of remorse. They shock to inoculate against sterner shocks, full of remorse all the while. I brought Tzdze onto the balcony and unknowingly gave her that stark shock, that amounts to showing her how things stood then, better that than allow Wite to come to her directly. I took Tzdze out onto the balcony without any reservation. In the room off the hall where Tzdze had sat to supervise the servants, Tzdze taught me my lesson, showed me how things stood with her then, and it was my turn to be tortured. My uncle Heckler tortured me. Torture can only teach you how to be tortured. The torture that comes later is a test and a reminder. There's no civilization without this well-meaning torture, it is *the cornerstone of civilization*, I will never accept it I will never be reconciled to it, to hell with it! I ignored my hateful good sense and fell down in front of Tzdze's chair and begged her with tears in my eyes not to refuse to see me precisely in order to make the torture worse, to show Tzdze more suffering than she wanted to cause, or to satisfy her—not enough. Even Tzdze wasn't above reckoning whether or not I was suffering *enough*, and of course everyone reckons the suffering they endure and the suffering they mete out like this, they can't help but be unfair; there's no getting away from transactions of suffering like this, people reckon how much they suffer and how much suffering they mete out in a secretive little economy where each new smart loses its peculiar character and joins the rest in a completely vague succession of injuries; no one actually reckons up debits and credits in suffering, but at every new smart a legion of old tortures are resurrected and their shades go out to meet it and compound it, give us a feeling we have a debt to discharge. Each new smart loses its peculiar character and discharges itself on some other undeserving person, and so on and on like money. I can only hope that Tzdze will remember what I did and see clearly how I was tortured, and finally forgive me. Tzdze is the only one whose forgiveness I want. Only Tzdze could understand, and Tzdze is the only one whose understanding I want. Tzdze will never read this. I will find her soul when I'm dead. This is idle talk. This is only *idle talk*. My uncle Heckler thought he tortured me for my own good, this was his way of being a "good Alak." The Alaks especially torture their subjects with a sad face, full of remorse, they *sincerely* torture their subjects. They overran the world with open arms. They buried and prayed over each one they killed, with tears. My guards here are apologetic, they wanted me to move to the infirmary and when I refused they said they would "honor my wishes." My two guards nurse me with more concern than I ever had from my family. I've never had so much attention. If I wasn't dying they would certainly have hanged me by now, but even so with unpretended grief and a funeral. What will my guards do without me? Certainly find a new sick old man. No one gets past them. If I asked them to despise me, they might, out of respect. I'm glad to know that my so-called countrymen and some others here want me executed right away, out in the street, but there is no doubt at all that there is not one Alak among them, and that not one Alak or Alak representative would listen to them. The Alaks are as if all of one mind; there's no hate in them, but they are indestructably hard. They are ruthless especially when they are respectful. Ruthless respect is the Alak's secret weapon.

I was ruthless from the start, but my uncle Heckler and the Alaks made me more ruthless. Wite and Tzdze both were and are utterly ruthless as am I within my limitations. From the start I loved ruthlessness, my uncle Heckler's ruthlessness of thought was overpowering—I learned to think that way with real joy, stark and rigorous as Wite and Tzdze. I didn't want to fail them. My wife was ruthless within her limitations, she was like me. I feel nothing but impatience and despair when I'm surrounded by flaccid helpless city people. Shapeless confused lives of flaccid helpless city people carrying on flaccid every day every day as shapeless and confused as the next and that will last from day to day forever to the grave and beyond with, at the very best, a moment or two that had accidentally taken some shape.

I can be driven to desperation by the soft press of those shapeless confused lives, I've been driven out of every city in the world by the soft press of helpless confused flaccid city people. I've been driven out or worn out or pushed all around in every city in history—I pushed myself out of that *living human quicksand*. I did everything in my power to escape and undo the living human quicksand of the cities. My eyes were only for looking at spirits, my uncle Heckler had trained them specifically *to see through human quicksand*.

I left Tzdze, rose to my feet all at once and left the house for the last time, directly. When I came out from the hedges I was struck by the full light of the sun for the first time in days. For the first time in days the sky was clear, the shadow cast by the hedge had a sharp edge—I knew exactly when I passed out of it and the full light of the sun fell on me, directly in view of the mountain and cave and the stone outbuilding and in full view of Wite when I emerged from the hedges, leaving Tzdze's house for the last time. I didn't know where I was going yet, Wite was waiting to tell me. I left without knowing where I was going and rode toward the trees through the clearing. The horse was only walking—this *weird happiness* came into me, with something like a click I was euphoric from out of confusion and fluttering everywhere inside me there was *weird happiness* that made the world shake and grow thin. The world looked as if it were stretched thin over something bright. There's no way to make you understand this, my head was all empty except for this *weird happiness* that had pushed out everything else. Even in full view of the house, mountain, cave, the stone outbuilding, in full view really of Wite and Tzdze, whom I had just left forever, this euphoria overcame me out of nothing. I don't want to make a mystery out of something simple—all I mean is that this sudden feeling made my head swim, even what I'd just been through with Tzdze, that scene, seemed charming and small from where I was standing, all at once I was elevated even on level ground and I seemed to see the whole story in one piece as easy to grasp as anything directly in front of me would be, like a ball tossed into my hand. I didn't see anything, nothing I couldn't have seen or remembered normally, there was nothing new except a sense that I was spread out in connection to every moment and you could say "touching everything." I was directly touching everything there all at once. The *weird happiness* was a kind of world-lighting feeling but I know my head was only swimming, no one can see anything that isn't there, there's no depth to look further into, my head was swimming, I felt euphoria attached to whatever occurred to me, it was the light I looked with. What I want to say is that there was nothing *else* in that *weird happiness*, it didn't go anywhere, there was no miracle. Wite wasn't causing anything to happen inside me.

Going out for him, knowing that I was going to do what he told me to do, that was what caused it. It wasn't mysterious, it was confusing. I left Tzdze's house in full view of them both and the woods closed around me—that finished it.

CHAPTER TEN

———

If Wite hadn't come back what difference would it have made, Tzdze and I saw him and knew Wite had come back, Wite had never left, but even if Wite hadn't been there to be seen Tzdze and I would have seen him, Tzdze and I couldn't fail to see him everywhere because he was in our eyes already, Wite was branded into our eyes so that even if Wite wasn't there to be seen *we* would still be seeing Wite. Our memories would have supplied Wite to our senses lacking Wite as an object; we were not *accustomed* to seeing Wite, no once could have accustomed himself to seeing Wite, he didn't persist for us out of *habit*, he came at Tzdze and came at me at will, out of Tzdze's memory and my memory, without any remembering. Wite was not dead for Tzdze and me, Wite was not dead to the world or to himself. Genuinely dead, lost, people of whom me say "*our* dead," will endure in living memory; Wite was not dead or lost, not confined to living memory, Tzdze and I did not strictly speaking remember him, Wite was something else entirely, he was no phantom memory, he was no phantom supposition like a living acquaintance either, Wite was not properly presented to our senses but he was no plain memory no dream no delirium Wite was not a "mental state" Wite was no "mental process," Wite is here *immediately*. Wite is *immediately* at my side—he is *at my side*, not *in my head* he is *at my side. Almost nothing* has changed since Wite "died." *I* have changed more than Wite.

The first people I came across I watched for days without letting on that I was there, I was content to be their bogeyman and spy on them or simply watch them without probing. I watched them go to and fro, every day to and fro, where they lived all together by a half-buried flat boulder in a clearing with a well and a big barn and a two hundred pound bell on a wooden scaffold. They hit the bell with a mallet to parse out the day, it was far too heavy to ring with a cord, its bronze was three inches thick. I watched them for days and I had no idea what I was looking at: they were creatures, I didn't understand anything they did. I watched them for days without knowing what they were, nothing they were doing made sense. For days I watched them and I never once could make sense of them or find anything to say about them, xcept that they went to and fro, worked, ate, and rang the bell. Days passed, I continued to hide in the woods and watch them mystified.

I was mystified by them. They fascinated me. I was disturbed and mystified, ready to be content with them if I could only settle somewhere on who they were, ready to be content simply with watching them; but I had to tell them about Wite. Wite had instructed me to tell people about him, and I was going to do it. They were so incomprehensible, these creature people I mean, I couldn't even begin to rack my brains about a way to tell them about Wite—*that* was a question that couldn't be asked. They came and went, and I watched them and learned nothing, I watched them thoughtlessly. They delved in the ground during the day and busied themselves around the barn at night, and rang the bell. Wherever they went they would all go together, they were always bunched together like a gaggle of geese. Once I did look around the barn, when they were all out in the field. I went through some of their things, a huge pile of incomprehensible things. Long before the bell rang them in from the field I had hidden myself away again. The bell would ring them in from the field, they rambled back in a knot as always, with the big farmer in the center. No matter what, the big farmer was always in the midst of them, he was the first I could single out from them. The second was his unmarried sister-in-law—I hadn't noticed at first but she never went with them, she had to stay behind and ring the bell.

She was invisible, she vanished the moment they left and appeared only to ring the bell. The moment that knot of them returned she disappeared in their midst. I never could figure out where she went. When I knew their habits I could get closer to them. The big farmer's unmarried sister-in-law vanished on her own before I dared go down to look at their incomprehensible piles of goods. I learned all their patterns of coming and going and little else until I got close enough. There was next to nothing to know since they went in the morning and came in the evening every day without stopping, without variation, forever the same business filling every day, and eventually I could get closer to them, while they were working. They were always oblivious to anything but each other and their work, they never went past each other and their work. I got close enough to hear them speak and make out their words. I didn't understand, it dawned on me that I didn't know their language, it dawned on me with tremendous relief that we wouldn't be able to speak to each other, that they wouldn't be able to speak their work-every-day-the-same language at me, and I wouldn't be forced to listen to them speak out of their work-every-day-the-same lives. All of a sudden it was easy, I waited for them in the road. I left my things by the flat boulder in the clearing and waited. The bell rang behind me, soon I could see the knot coming toward me. They rushed forward when they saw me and came up around me, they knotted me in with them and stared at me, ever since I met Wite I've looked especially horrible. More and more like a walking cadaver every day, and these earthy people were knotted in on all sides of me without speaking—I looked from one face to another. One by one I turned around and looked from one face to another, I wanted to make some gesture to them but I couldn't even raise my arms along my body without shoving against them—some invisible gesture from the big farmer towering over us all set the knot moving and I was borne along with it. I had room to move and I began gesturing at them; for nothing, because they were all staring at me but staring without actually paying attention, or paying me the worst kind of attention, not the sort of attention one gives to a person, even a stranger is a recognisable *person*. They stared while I waved my arms at them, I was trying to get them to look back down the road, toward Wite's mountain just visible over the trees. They waved back and me and smiled, pointing down the road in imitation of me, staring at me without stopping. We arrived in the clearing by the bell and they stopped around me, staring and smiling and mimicking my gestures, thrusting their malicious smiling stares right in my face and imitating me while I tried to get the big farmer's attention. No one spoke. The big farmer's unmarried sister-in-law came around the bell and joined her smiling staring face to the others' and she imitated their imitations. The big farmer was the only one who hadn't imitated me or smiled at me.

He had left the knot at once and opened the barn doors. He called them inside and they brought me along, staying close in around me and grinning. I was deposited in a corner while they went about their business, always staring and grinning at me, turning their heads away to chatter with each other and turning them back to me, getting ready to play new games with me—I tried to get the big farmer's attention. They instantly flickered their hands as I was waving mine and mewling over my voice when I tried to speak, a number of them noticed me speaking and rushed to me babbling syllables back to me. They called the big farmer, calling him Felix, of all things, and he stood and stared at me again, over their heads. They were cooing and muttering at me and wringing their hands in imitation of me; presently a lump of bread was produced somehow, and Felix watched them hold it out to me and snatch it back again and again.

I got to my feet and began again, pointing out the open door and even forcing my way through them to point directly to Wite's mountain, I said "Wite" and they who were all pointing already and staring at me said "Wite" back through their grins staring at me. Felix watched. I felt weak and suddenly nearly fainting with dizziness. They caught me and carried me to the corner, laid me down on the hay and hovered over me grinning and saying "Wite" every now and then. I was sure Felix the big farmer understood me, why I don't know, and I tried to call him or get up but I was forever pushed gently down. They would yell "Felix" over their shoulders in my tone of voice, and with the same subtle mispronounciation, and then say "Wite" to me. Sometimes I would look past their heads and see Felix standing over them, staring down at me, I knew he understood me when I spoke. I fell back in weakness and frustration over and over again.

I closed my eyes and came and went, every time I opened my eyes one or another of them would be staring grinning down at me only inches from my face, and I would start weakly and try to wave the face away, wave them off. They would imitate me and more would join them from other parts of the barn, even while I got the impression that most of them were by then asleep. Felix, or whatever his name really was, was nowhere to be seen, one or two were staying up with me, taking turns hovering like an anchor on top of me, pawing my chest and shoulder a little sometimes to wake me, so I would give them something else of mine to imitate. They tormented me until the bell called them outside. Daylight was everywhere, I bounded up and saw them filing outside, smelled the food they'd been eating a moment before. The place was stifling with bad air

and cooking smells. I looked everywhere for Felix, he turned up immediately in front of me with a mattock in his hands—he held it out to me,
the knot of them watched silently staring and grinning. I pushed it back
and pointed over their heads to Wite's mountain, they imitated. I started
talking to Felix and was immediately drowned out by their voices. Felix
pushed the mattock at me and let go, I let it drop. Felix was turning but
turned back and picked up the mattock. Felix threw the mattock to me,
I caught it and threw it down, pointing and trying to make myself heard
over the uproar. Felix thrust me into the knot and suddenly I was with
him in the middle being dragged to the field. They brought me with them
to the field, Felix pushed the mattock into my arms and I let it fall and
tried to make myself heard, Felix looked at me. I spent that day dragged
up and down the field with them as they worked, they didn't ignore me,
they worked *at* me without stopping, they never broke off work or missed
a day in the field, they worked endlessly, today they worked *at* me, smiling
and staring when they could, I had to stay on my feet all day exhausted
and starving as I was and they were nudging me out of their way forever,
leaving me no peace, never letting up on me but forever nudging me to
this side, nudging me to that side, pushing me a little back out of their
way, pushing me a little forward out of their way, drudging back and forth
all around me with a little push and then a nudge this way, pushing me
this way and then nudging me back again, adjusting me every moment,
without letting up, I tried to speak at least to Felix, or whatever his name
was, but what good did it do me to try? The tools would hammer against
the ground and the knot of them would cackle like chickens echoing my
voice, my calls to Felix, chattering "Wite" back at me when they had nothing else to say, I would open my mouth and the cackling would surge up
over my voice and drown me every time, I couldn't make myself heard. I
only wanted to fall over into the dirt and let them cover me over or plough
me under if they liked, they would do as they pleased, they knew nothing
past that, I already knew, I somehow was determined to tell Felix anyway,
I was determined to tell Felix, if no one else, because he could follow what
I said, that I believed I was certain. I was sure he would understand me
if I could only tell him. I spent that day dragged up and down their nev-
erendingly overturned field, until the bell struck and the knot cinched in
around me, Felix just behind me, they carried me back with them. Again

Felix went off and opened the doors for them, then I all at once rushed at him, I was all at once too fast for them, I seized Felix by the arm and pulled him inside, I shut the one open door behind us, I shut the knot of them out for a moment and they piled up against the windows, Felix was glaring at me and trying to get around me.

He pulled his arm every time from my grasp, I was already fixing him with my eyes and starting to talk directly into his face, I spoke clearly and directly into Felix's face so that even Felix, or whatever his name was, who had never been fixed like this and spoken to so directly, had to stop and listen, he was helpless not to listen, Felix listened because I could speak so that he must listen, at least when he and I were alone inside the barn with the others shut out. When he was naked without them, I told Felix about Wite in the mountain, I didn't waste time, I didn't tell Felix anything like the whole story, I told Felix what was essential, what was at stake, I *warned* Felix about Wite, I told Felix who Wite was. Felix, who had never been spoken to so directly, understood what I was saying. He listened. There was no doubt of that. He fell back from me but he listened and clearly he understood, because he paused, Felix seemed bewildered, and the racket that had been bustling outside, at the windows, fell off, when they saw him pull back from me and saw that he seemed bewildered by what I said. They hadn't understood me but they were watching Felix. Soon it was quiet and Felix, or whatever his name really was, seemed to notice that they were watching him. I didn't detain him when he went to open the door, Felix went outside, the knot gathered around him without speaking. Felix turned and beckoned me outside, I went outside, Felix looked at me, Felix asked me, "Where are your things?" I pointed to the flat boulder by the well, the boulder was half-buried and I had dropped my bag there behind it and tied my horse near to it, Felix told me "Get them." I went over to the boulder, this was the first time I'd been apart from them since I'd come, it felt strange and wonderful to be able to move so freely and without forcing my way against a sort of blizzard of abuse, and picked up my bag. I turned to face them and looked I suppose expectantly at Felix, Felix had just picked up a rock and he threw it at me, it hit me in my head. I suppose it knocked me down. I suppose it knocked me unconscious for a few moments.

My head was swimming, I couldn't get up for a few minutes, I don't think I did fall unconscious. When I got to my feet the sky was already almost completely dark.

The sky was almost completely dark, I was getting to my feet and even though the sky was clear it was getting dark, Wite's mountain hadn't moved but it seemed to swell until it blocked the sun, everyone stopped when this happened and looked up, there was a burst of thunder from the mountain and the sky darkened, the wind came up all at once and the bell starting ringing by itself loud regular peals that set its heavy edges humming and jerked it a little side to side without jangling it or breaking the regular rhythm of its shouts, everyone watched it and flinched with each loud peal—Felix whipped back and spun falling on his stomach in the hay, he turned onto his side holding his shoulder, I saw a stain spreading beneath his fingers, Felix was staring at a rock lying a few inches away from his nose, he raised himself on an elbow and looked wildly around recoiled as another rock struck his chest knocking him flat on his back. He rolled over and started scrabbling toward the barn, a rock cracked against one of his knees and he screamed and faltered, a heavy rock flew out from between the trees where no one was and curved in the air arcing down and crushing his hip, Felix screamed as loud as the bell and I saw him drive his fingers into the ground, everyone else had screamed when they saw where the big stone flew out and Felix had turned to stare over his shoulder, a rock shot out from the trees and broke his skull, everyone was trying to pull away from him but something kept the knot together in that spot, rocks the size of apples, and larger, streamed past me in all directions toward them but they were stuck together in one mob around Felix's fallen body, more and more and the rocks were flying faster and faster and getting smaller and smaller whizzing past me like bullets, I turned my head and a black cloud of rocks too dense to see through shot past me and tore them all to shreds punched apart the barn behind them so that it listed forward and collapsed in splinters, the knot was a huge red heap, the boulder behind me rose in the air as if it were a dead leaf and flew over my head gaining speed and it smashed into the remains of the barn flying straight through and stopping in just above the treeline instantly rising and flying back moving smoothly and erratically in the grip of an invisible hand up into the air and then pounding them into the ground, rising up with gore and slamming down harder and harder. The bell stopped and the boulder lay half-buried in the ground in a pile of pulverized rocks, the ruins of the barn behind it with the dust still rising.

I had been holding my head. The bleeding had already stopped. The sky was as bright as it had been before. Near me, Felix's unmarried sister-in-law lay bawling on the ground by the well with her hands screwed over her eyes. She had not joined in with the rest of them immediately when they came back, she had been somewhere else. Without saying anything to her I collected my things by the torn spot where the boulder had been and left immediately. I went to find my horse where I'd tied it. How blue the light from my window is getting. When the trees closed around me I remember the humid air cooled my exposed blood, where my scalp had been cut. The air between the trees cooled my exposed blood and refreshed me a little.

I can go on without thinking, with one step. Once I've stepped to one side I can keep going, days are going by, I'm travelling, the trees are drifting by me. I travelled from place to place, I may have dreamt all that travelling, the trees drifted around me, I saw that time was passing. Now my memories are getting tangled, I'm drawing everything out without inflection, you will get everything I have once I've drawn it out, if this is my will then I will you this testimony, you'll understand why at the end. When the end comes, if I haven't worked for nothing—I almost said "worked so hard"—if I haven't worked for nothing you're going to understand why I'm willing this to you by the end, you will know that you understand if you can do it yourself. You can believe what you like and do whatever you want. You'll know you understand when you do it yourself. Wite isn't interested—let them believe whatever they like and do whatever they want, as long as they know about Wite. Tell them about Wite, and *then* let them do what they want! What will they want *then?* You'll know if you understand when you do it yourself, when Wite says "show me you understand," and you show him.

I remember everything drifting like snow on all sides of me, blue light and trees. I never got tired of being surrounded by trees. I visited a spot between some low hills something smaller than a valley that was I'm sure the moistest spot in the forest, without being boggy, it wasn't sodden but the air was so dewy I could feel the fluid condensing in my lungs from breathing it. That was the moistest spot in the forest, it was in among a bundle of low hills that flattened out around the waterlogged palisade of a town I'll call Kursick; I was there in the early morning—there were already some people here and there around the treeline, mostly children with a few older brothers and sisters superintending; they were gathered at the treeline and just a little in among the trees collecting blue gills of fungus, they do this in the early morning when the air is moistest to keep the spores from getting everywhere, nothing can float in the air early in the morning, the air is too heavy for anything to float in it. At any other time of day the spores would get everywhere, after a few minutes the air would be unbreathable, too full of spores. The air is so dewy in the early morning that it's safe even for children to go out and gather the gills. They'll bring them back to Kursick, their parents will pulp the gills and make a paste out of them, and ferment the paste. The people in the town eat almost nothing but this appalling fermented blue paste, both in Kursick and other towns around there, I've never tasted it but it smells like old pickle jars. They eat mounds of fermented paste stinking of old pickle jars well into old age and then are dragged off to their graves packed in blue clay and stinking of old pickle jars. Imagine the deadly monotony of a thousand generations of sodden old paste-chewing people in Kursick and neighboring towns, sending out the children every morning to haul in more. The graves of thousands of generations past sprout fresh blue gills for the good people of Kursick and neighboring towns to suck. There was a constellation of children strung out around and just within the treeline collecting those blue gills in baskets, and one boy I noticed was doing terribly, pulling the gills off in pieces and dropping the bits all around his feet, this boy couldn't be bothered to pay attention to what he was doing, he was wasting his time, he couldn't pay attention to those blue gills and why should he? Who could be expected to pay attention? The boy pulled at the gills once and a while and stood stupidly in place, once and a while he would look to this side or that with a completely mindless expression on his face, he clearly went without sleep, he looked exhausted. The expression on his face was painful to look at, a child's face magnifies everything, it was easy to see how exhausted and worn-out he was even from a distance, it was almost immediately apparent, I noticed his exhaustion almost before I noticed him in particular. The boy pulled at the gills with no attention, while I should have been invisible to them all he surely noticed me, he surely gave me all of his attention. The boy was looking directly at me even though I should have been invisible to all of them. He had stopped and had been standing looking stupidly down at his feet, then he looked out around him with abandon and at once he locked eyes with me. After a while I wanted to make some gesture and get his attention or call attention to what he was doing to himself, because he was looking at me without a thought in his head, like an animal, with nothing but silence in his head I'm sure, I know how he seemed to me, he looked at me like an animal with nothing but silence in his head and there I was in his silence staring mindlessly back at him from behind a tree where I was hiding. I wanted to remind him of himself because one of his older sisters was getting ready to bother him about the gills, because he wasn't picking any, she pinched his shoulder and he spun around and began picking again at once without saying anything or turning to look at me again. He was pinching at the gills tearing out little bits and tossing them down toward the basket without looking. I didn't know what to do. I didn't want to be pointed out, although I didn't think he was about to point me out to anyone; I retreated back a little into the woods, but I took no special pains to be quiet and I didn't take any special pains not to be seen, although I wasn't. I went back into the woods and sat. It's on this boy's account, because he is still alive and free, that I won't give his town its proper name, I call it Kursick at random, the Alaks won't get the name of his hometown from me.

That night, when I passed that way a second time, I saw someone coming, although it was late, the stockade—there was a stockade surrounding the town, what in the world they had to defend I couldn't imagine, but perhaps it was to keep people in—the stockade was shut up for the night and the lights were all doused, that same boy was running through the clearing toward the trees. I couldn't see clearly though I could see more clearly than most in that light, I saw the bruised expression on his face, he was running, it was clearly him, he ran to the treeline and stopped on the ground, by the roots, under cover. I couldn't see him through the bracken and I started looking for him as quietly as I could. I pawed my way down through the bracken toward the spot where I had last seen the boy, the spot at the treeline where he had vanished under cover, and after a moment I could hear him, his breath was coming in short gasps, a little faint, and sometimes his voice would pass through, he gasped or moaned at intervals. I remember I had been looking for some amount of time and listening to his little faint pants and gasping, when I saw that what I had been taking, at the corner of my eye, for a patch of light from the moon, was, when I looked directly, the boy's chest, I hadn't expected his shirt to be open but he was lying on his back propped up against the roots, his shirt was open and I had been taking his little ribs for a patch of light from the moon. I could see him clearly, and when I saw him, he was holding his arm and only just noticing me. I came up closer, his face was turning a bit green and he was holding his right hand, his whole body—his body was still pretty small—his whole body was rigid and shaking with pain. I came right up over him, he smelled like burnt toast.

I saw—they had broken his hand. I reached and fixed it at once—I was still able to do that, nothing had changed. I don't know what I did then, I only stood around, probably not sure what to do. Children almost always make me nervous, they're so fragile that only a moment's awkwardness can damage them. I'm most afraid of causing *invisible damage*, one thoughtless word . . . It's hard not to resent children for being as vulnerable as they are, it's a whole separate effort not to blame them for being as vulnerable as they are, I never knew what to do with my son or what I was doing with a son in the first place, a person like me has no business bringing more sufferers into the world let alone raising one, *imparting my knowledge of life to it*! There's no point in trying to impart knowledge of life to children, there's nothing any adult can tell a child about how to live that they could possibly understand, at best an adult can equip a child with prejudices that way, sow the seeds of confusion as I'm sure I did, sow the seeds of disillusionment as I'm sure I did, there's no imparting wisdom to children. The only thing I ever taught my son was how to hate me. I did it unwillingly and without knowing that I was teaching him to hate me, but it was my only unique personal contribution to his upbringing. I think my wife's only unique personal contribution to his upbringing had been that she taught him to hate her as well and for much the same reasons. He was a good boy. We were happy with him when he was young, but as he grew older he turned his back every day a little bit more from both of us and left the moment he didn't need us any more. He wouldn't have anything to do with us, neither of us knew why he left, there was no chance for anything more to happen, because he wouldn't speak to us any more. After my wife died, I learned that he had gone to live with my family to spite me. I'm sure they were happy to have him, to spite me. I'm sure they took him to heart and cherished him as a *real member of the family* to spite me and in spite of me. Spite toward me was the common family trait that brought them together. This boy in the cover by the treeline was nothing like my son as far as I could tell then. He was looking between me and his perfectly unbroken hand, I was not looking directly at him, I was not giving him any reason to think I wanted anything from him. I could see, peripherally, that he was trying to ask me several questions at once, or that he was trying to think of something to say. This was taking too long so I left. He came after me and told me that he didn't want to go back—he asked me if I expected him to go back. I said I didn't expect him to do anything, but that it would make sense if he didn't want to go back. I still remember this conversation, by some miracle. He asked how I thought he'd broken his hand. I told him I was sure he'd had his hand broken for him. He asked me what I'd done to his hand. I told him that his hand was really no longer broken, that the effect was permanent. He asked me what I had done *exactly* to his hand again. I said that I was a spirit-eater. He didn't know what a spirit-eater was so I explained that to him and answered a number of other unimportant questions, I gave him my name and he gave me his, a name you won't get from me—instead I'll call him Tamt, which was my wife's dead brother's name. Tamt is alive and still free, as far as I know, and I'm sure that Alaks know about him already without reading any of this, they're already searching for him—I won't have them learn anything from me. When I told Tamt I was traveling, Tamt had thought I was living in the woods outside Kursick, he asked me a number of questions about where I was going, I eventually told him I was probably heading to Lohach, he kept on asking questions until I sheepishly understood what he was doing and invited him to join me, Tamt agreed. Tamt agreed to come with me without hesitating. He was my good boy.

I asked Tamt who had seen him run off, he said no one had, he'd waited until they were all asleep. I told Tamt, that when his people missed him in the morning, they'd start searching. They'd search until they were satisfied, as long as they cared, then decide he was dead and give up—I asked Tamt if he wanted them to imagine him dead. Tamt said no. I told him to let them know. I think I said, "If you don't want them to think you ran *off* you have to show them you've run *away*." After one moment Tamt picked up a branch and ran to the treeline. He started battering the blue gills off the trees. In no time he'd pried all the blue gills off the trunks and trampled them to bits. When Tamt finished he came up to me, breathing hard. His eyes were shining at me and he was breathing hard through his grinning mouth. I remember standing there in front of him in the shadows of the trees and getting an idea. It took a long time, but I got an idea and asked Tamt how they grew the gills. He said they would chop at the bark here and there, near the roots of the trees, and the spores would set in the gaps. Did the spores always need a break in the bark? I asked. "Yes," Tamt said. I now had a complete idea. I went down to one of the trees and knelt by it, with its trunk in my two hands down by the roots where the bark was broken and there were blue scars where Tamt had ripped the gills off, and I fixed the bark so that it came up solid from the ground, without a chink and hard as rock. Tamt saw what I did, he saw at once that I was ruining that tree for the purposes of growing blue gills of fungus. I knelt and fixed the bark, and I could see right through to the heart of the wood, I saw the spirit there, it was vast. It was thinner than tissue and slow, vast, it noticed me so slowly I could see the little shimmer, that was its noticing, go along its length. I was kneeling and the bark was coming up and growing solid, and then I felt Wite come up. He just came up out of nothing all around me, this was a feeling like standing in the water when a wave rolls by and lifts you a bit, then broadly pulls you rushing on all sides until you don't know whether you're standing still or moving, I went to the shore once with my wife and was terrified, especially when I stood in the water with the waves coming all around me, Wite was coming up around me out of nothing, through the earth. When I looked here and there, after I stood up, I saw that all the trees had solid bark coming up from the roots, sometimes as high as the lower branches, the bark was solid, without a chink and hard as rock. Tamt was looking at me. He saw what had happened and he wasn't sure about me. I remember it being quiet, a few crickets. I offered Tamt my hand and he took it at once. Tamt and I left and went back into the forest. When the sun started to come up, much later, we hadn't spoken, we'd been going over rough ground and we both had been picking our way in the dark. When the sun came up, I saw a low hill and had another thought. I turned and looked at Tamt. We had been awake all night, moving very fast through the forest, Tamt's eyes were glassy from lack of sleep and stared back at me, but he was grinning, he was filled with vitality, and I was in exactly the same state, I'm sure I glanced at him with glassy, bulging eyes and a grinning, alert face. I felt full of heady, weightless energy, my eyes were extra open and everything seemed especially bright, the air felt sharper, I was exhausted and nearly panicking with energy at the same time, and Tamt was the same as me, at the same time. We had both looked at each other the same way at the same time, with glassy eyes, exhausted and nearly panicking with energy. I wanted Tamt to come with me to the top of the hill. From there, I showed him Wite's mountain. It was towering over the trees. I pointed directly at the cave. I told Tamt everything, I told him about Wite, I saw a glint from the mountain while I was telling him about Wite and I saw his eyes were brimming, every word fell through their transparency and struck root in his head, I looked up at the mountain and saw the glinting from the slope, then a sound boomed from the woods between us, between the mountain and our hill, the sound boomed from the woods, as if the trees were all living horns—its tone rose and fell, it was so loud I could feel the air rumbling and the air seemed to become clearer still—the hair was raising all over my head, I was paralyzed, the sound was rising and falling over our heads, coming from the woods, now and then it would stop and I would hear its echoes disappearing, and I would feel my body go a little slack and my hair fall flat—then it would come back and I would be paralyzed again—this went on and on. It was Wite acknowledging me and Tamt, my first convert. Tamt was converted then. Things were started growing then, with Tamt. But that sound was also the trees and the mountain *addressing us directly.* Imagine being addressed directly by a mountain! It poured out on us like sunlight, while the sun rose. Imagine being *directly addressed* by nature. The sound was so loud it nearly knocked me down, it came from everywhere. Wite was one of the elements, like the weather, he wasn't anything like a person anymore. He'd made himself into an element. I was going to bring him from there, to every city in the world.

CHAPTER ELEVEN

———

Let me tell you why directly. If you don't understand you never will. I was sustained through everything by my fancy that the whole world will end, my days have at least beaten that into me without knowing it, every time the next day struck me I fell more in love with the end of the world, I've loved it more and more. I've come to depend on it, the end of the world is something I look forward to, and that I imagine often, with great pleasure. The end of the world exists, it is present immediately. It is touching every moment, so to speak it's standing outside the door every moment, it could come in at any moment. I depend absolutely on that, for the wherewithal to draw my next shallow imperfect breath, like any hopeless person would, but there is more in the end of the world than an idea for me, because I've seen Wite. The whole of the world at long last no more, there's no imagining it. I went to Lohach with a picture in my head of a completely ruined city, nothing but rubble, all my life I've been drawn and drawn to ruins, I've pictured everything around me in fresh ruin, I imagine a city freshly ruined, and see all the everyday faces changed, the citizens wander around in a daze, stripped naked by the ruination of their city, they have nothing to say to each other, they can't speak, they can't desire, they're barren, crippled, they have nothing. I wanted to live inside those ruins and make nothing out of them, without so much as shifting a few planks to patch the holes in the roof, not so much as picking up a broom to sweep away the broken glass—leave it, let it lacerate my foul hateful feet. Leave the clutter in the streets, let the city go down as it is, where there's nothing to be done, nowhere to go, nothing moving, no business, no conversation, no inanities, only silence and resignation. Let them know, and leave them nothing. Throw them down. A full stop to everyday business, the ruination of the city, that is the only completion that can be hoped for, or that should be hoped for. It's the only hope that isn't an obscene hope. A ruined city is the only sort of city I could live in. I could walk to and fro, one place looking much the same as any other, just piles of rubble, and I could meet people in the street and in the ruins, and feel at home with them, when it didn't matter any more who they were supposed to be. Who we are would also be in ruins, and our language would be ruined and just barely intelligible. They wouldn't be anybody, that's how I would resemble them. We would all be at the mercy of the elements, all the same—that's what I want to bring to every city in the world, I want to see every city in the world ruined like that, every abominable family, church, army, hanging in rags, all those abominable groupings of people smashed to pieces, leaving only the handful of permanently stupefied survivors and debris as far as the eye can see. All I wanted—although I loved Tzdze, and at the same time it seems more and more idiotic that I should bother to speak of wanting and loving—all I wanted was to see the end of the world. Wite selected me and sent me instructions, and I was a willing instrument, I am Wite's willing instrument, to bring about the end. Wite has made himself into an element, Wite will strike blindly and follow in my wake where I go, here and there wherever I go, and bring down whatever has been built up there. You must understand that he will act blindly, with no more reasoning or totting up of plans than a fire. Tzdze will survive unharmed with Wite's protection, I love her and for that reason say nothing to Tzdze, I go away, nothing will change for Tzdze though the world may end, don't imagine I've forgotten her. You may think I'm weak and tired and resentful, and you're entirely right, but even though I admit shamelessly to babbling here like a half wit I will insist to the end that I am not inventing and I am not tailoring circumstance to please me. But even if I were, what business is that of yours? Are you so honest? Tzdze was no more in the world than I, and she will be safe even if I am not kept safe—why should I be kept safe? Do I care so much what happens to me? Let the wall cave in and crush me this moment. Tzdze will be spared, as I know, and that's all—

I went to Lohach on Wite's instructions. Tamt and I walked in the road like regular people and eventually we found a coach-road and followed it, Tamt on my horse and I on the ground leading them both. My horse was ailing, it was moving slower every day, it seemed only to want to rest, I could never tell what an animal was thinking, what its gestures meant, I decided it was either too sick or too old, or too tired, and I released it in one of the last few wild spots before the coach station at Klosdanz.

Wearily it sauntered into the woods and disappeared. I hated to take the coach but there was no going on with that horse, it had finished. For all I know, it's still there in the woods near Klosdanz, roving in the trees foraging. Or lying flattened into the ground like a leather satchel, a feast for worms. Tamt and I released him in a wild spot and walked into Klosdanz. I didn't think anyone would recognise me there, the station was attached to a greasy little inn, neither Tamt nor I had any desire to "refresh" ourselves in there, I think we got hold of some dried cherries somewhere and ate those, waiting for the coach. Nothing could have been more strange than to stand there as I did, eating *cherries*, of all things, so dry as to be virtually without flavor but nevertheless, after that it began to seem that anything was possible. I looked forward to the coach ride with dread, I've always hated coaches, I've always hated anything that thrusts strange people right under my nose, ever since my first coach ride to the capital, when I left my uncle Heckler. Tamt and I took the coach when it came and had the seat to ourselves, I remember the appalling people sitting opposite us, I remember sitting there helpless in the dank, humid air inside the coach, helplessly breathing their air, I spent the whole trip hammered back into my seat by an endless soliloquy, one of the passengers was soliloquizing to another in a so-called foreign language, I could hear him inside the coach when it pulled up to collect us at the station, he soliloquized continuously without pausing for breath from Klosdanz to Lohach, yammering in a disgustingly liquid foreign language, without a single hard consonant, and at the top of his lungs, as if he were standing in a colossal amphitheatre and not sitting in that humid little box of misery, yammering in the full confidence of his kind that he naturally had every right to bleat out his shapeless words at the top of his lungs, without a thought in his head, like a machine; he would go on with his perfectly meaningless soliloquizing even if the world was ending around him, perhaps, if this isn't expecting too much, he might, at the last moment, suddenly look around him in complete disbelief, that there might be something in the world to stop him prattling on forever. Perhaps you think I'm no better, but I have a story to tell, and I don't go chewing it into the air for hours on end, where I'm not wanted. I have chosen to write my words in secret and in silence, so that I alone will hear them. Sometimes I imagine that you ask me how I could turn against the city, all the *humanity*, I imagine you bringing up this so-called *humanity*, I don't imagine you're trying to pass judgements on me, but I do imagine that you might not understand, and you'd bring up *humanity* as an *honest question*—whenever I think of *humanity* I think of that torture-oration I endured between Klosdanz and Lohach, I can't help but think of that reeking animal flapping his jaws in front of me for hours like a machine, and all the people like him, there are legions of identical copies of this one appalling specimen making life unbearable for numberless victims all over the world, I can only picture *humanity* as a mob of those orators and the wretches like me who are longing to put out our ears with hat pins—I love Tzdze, I love Wite, I love them more and more, and more and more, every instant my love for them grows, because they were inhuman, there was nothing of that chattering general character about them, they were *inhuman* and only *inhuman* things are worth loving—perhaps there are human things that cause me to feel love but they're not worth loving, I'm not sure they're worth loving, I'm not sure that I love those human failings, certainly not my own, and for others I think I can only be indulgent from time to time.

Not loving, but indulgent from time to time. By and large *humanity* means being buried alive in a humid little box of misery like that coach with a handful of human beasts heaped on top of you, the sweat dripping straight from the center of your forehead and the tip of your nose, your nose and mouth full up with human stink, feeling more desperate to escape every moment. I remember that bleak instant when I saw the trees falling away into the distance, I was completely out of place and alone without them, they fell away, I imagined the complacency with which the forest was regarded from the safety of the city, as something scenic. I watched the city rise up around me, as it closed around me, I remember how intense my desperation and disgust was—it peaked the moment we entered the main gate of Lohach, I saw the jumbled buildings all around me through the windows, Tamt and I watched them attack and eat up space on all sides, jumbled there at a bend in the Werse like a mass of rotting stuff clogging the river, and when I finally dragged myself out of the coach there was no relief, there was only more of the same on all sides; the air was just as rancid and stale, if not worse, for stinking with greater complication. Tamt and I couldn't rest, the noise and the stink were overwhelming, they wouldn't stop until we had been obliterated by them, the stink and the racket, I finally led Tamt to the Werse, not downstream where all the city's filth collects, becoming truly disastrous, but as far upstream as possible, by the first and second flood bridges, where the water flowed into Lohach from the woods too far away. Tamt and I were only able to catch our breath there in the middle of the second flood bridge, where the air was clean and a bit cooler, and there were very few people, and the forest was visible in the distance. That was the first place Tamt and I found rest, from there, we were able to go out into the city again after dark, when things grew more quiet, and the air a little fresher. Tamt and I were able to go back into the city, into Lohach, from the second flood bridge, only after dark, and we resumed searching the streets in complete silence, in the dark lanes, we took the empty streets from the second flood bridge into the empty lanes of the worst part of Lohach, Tamt and I made our way into the worst part of Lohach like a pair of bats, stealthy, silent, unseen, in utterly dark streets with buildings as tall as trees on either side of the lane, the buildings in this part of Lohach were left completely to the elements, they sagged out over the street or leant back away from the street, they were partially decomposed, every street smelling strongly of partially decomposed houses, but these houses would, I saw without much reflection, never fall over of their own accord—they needed to be *pushed*. We were there, in the worst part of Lohach, and there were a few others but they didn't notice us, Tamt and I kept to the stealthy streets and slipped past them all unseen. I wanted a brick building, without any special reason; I found a brick building and we set up house on the roof, inside the water tower. The building itself wasn't fit for us to live in but the water tower was ideal. Tamt and I weren't visible, there was an upright brick rampart screening us from the busier side of town, and we were high and near to the river, we could breathe. I had chosen the only brick building around—it was in the worst part of Lohach, but it was also right around the corner from the third city marketplace, which was by the river. We were in the worst part of the city, *and* right around the corner from the third marketplace.

Can you imagine that marketplace—in between the heaps of trash and the stalls; these stalls are always completely formless, these stalls are half-melted in appearance; in between them an endless stream of squat bawling housewives staggering up and down the aisles on their jointless legs, grossly inflated ankles, braying to each other at the top of their lungs, their deaf heads turning neither right nor left, their mouths hang open and as they never hear anything that's said to them from these open-hanging mouths they're forever groaning "-uh?" "-eh?" and they turn and bray that back and forth to each other. In the marketplace and throughout the city in Lohach there was almost nothing like my language, no recognizable language, what a hopeless pidgin these people made of my language! Here and there one might observe the atrocious guards with their moustaches, they were the most atrocious of the *male type* in Lohach, this impossible *male type* that is found everywhere and which must be utterly annihilated, the guards were gaseous red-faced Lohach men with moustaches, out of their inanimate eyes they would stand and glare impudently at each passerby out of their own undimensioned measure, out of their own undimensional measure *they* will judge *me*, let them condemn me in the worst possible terms, let me know with pride that they excoriate me with the most abysmal curses they can muster—I'll help them, I'll join my voice to theirs! Horrible horribly self-important men, the men at arms and the citizens, these self-important city jailors and impossible men with ideas of the world that stupidity must set far beyond the reach of discovery. I can't to this day imagine what idea such men might have of the world, except to say that it seems to me it must be hopeless, impossible to correct or to expand, they could not be more certain that their understanding of the world is *total*, they are certain that their hopeless, pitifully thin and watery notion of the world is *total*, they lack even the meager resources of mind to see that their hopeless, undimensioned, single-pointed notion of the world is not *total*—they admit of nothing else, they attack without provocation, they cannot be spoken to, they are too eager to feel their self-righteousness, to fall back on their paltry single-pointed certainty, whoever you are, they will come for you first, they are the ones to fear, and they own Lohach, Lohach is all theirs, it is the city that they built and it is the city that built them. *This is what comes of building cities.*

Tamt found our first convert in Lohach, the so-called third market blacksmith. He was not the bonded blacksmith. He had actually stolen his smithy from the bonded blacksmith in the third market, Tamt and I asked this person and that person—that is we asked the fruit seller, the glazier, and the butcher—who the third market blacksmith was. Tamt had drawn the blacksmith to my attention, because he was enormous even for a blacksmith, and because he was continually working and continually making mistakes. He barely sold anything, because he barely had anything worth selling. Tamt told me about him and drew him to my attention, I heard him long before I saw him. He struck everything he worked with such force that he could be heard a quarter of an hour before he was seen, he could be heard everywhere in that part of Lohach, even from our water tower. Tamt drew my attention to the sound in the morning, at the water tower, where I first heard it. The blacksmith barely made anything worth selling because he simply pounded away without any restraint and ruined everything he worked on, striking everything with such force he ended up battering his horseshoes and shovel blades and so forth all out of shape, he didn't think while he worked. He had too much force in him, or he couldn't hold himself back. Tamt pointed him out to me, the source of the sound I had heard from the water tower. He was enormous, and he struck his iron with so much force that sparks showered out onto the street, and sprayed across his face and his forearms, which were uncovered, although the sparks did not seem to scar him. His face and forearms were completely unscarred, even though they were regularly bathed in sparks from the forge. I watched him beat out a nameless thing, part of a carriage maybe, he struck it with more and more force, until finally he seized his long sledgehammer at its end and leaned over backwards until the sledgehammer's head grazed the ground behind him, at full length, and then swung it forward again with a stroke so swift I couldn't quite see it, the anvil groaned under the stroke and everyone within view, and Tamt and I, drew back sharply with the sudden and piercing sound, and the carriage part, or whatever it was, broke apart completely, its fragments, which were still glowing with heat, scattered across the floor, so that the floor and the walls smouldered where they fell, and the pieces smoked against the stones of the floor. The smith immediately went to find another piece of iron and began again, to produce, I suppose, another part of the same kind. I watched all this. Tamt and I began asking about him, we asked the fruit seller, the glazier, the butcher—they knew all about him, they had made up their minds about him years ago. We were told by the fruit seller that the smith had been an unwanted child, his parents hadn't wanted or named him, they called him "blunder." The glazier said, he was called "blunder" and had been sold by his parents to the bonded black-smith here, he had been a *slave* in that smithy. When the bonded black-smith died, "blunder" refused to leave the smithy, he drove off the bonded blacksmith's replacement, he forced the new smith to set up a stall at the other end of the third market (according to the butcher) because he re-fused to leave and couldn't be removed by force. "Blunder" was too strong to be removed by force, and he never left the smithy. What little he made well enough to sell, the butcher said, he traded for food, for iron, for fuel, and "blunder" never left his smithy. The bonded blacksmith had gone to the so-called authorities with his complaint but nothing was done about it, he had wanted to catch "blunder" at an off moment, out of the smithy, then seize hold of it. The bonded blacksmith imagined locking "blunder" out of the smithy, according to the butcher, but nothing came of it. The bonded blacksmith had more or less given all that up, according to the butcher, because "blunder" was no competition for him. "Blunder" struck the iron too hard and deformed almost everything he made uselessly.

Tamt and I took up with "blunder" effortlessly. He accepted us at once. I asked Tamt to look after "blunder"'s needs, to run and fetch whatever "blunder" needed. I designed a padlock for "blunder"'s smithy, so that he could leave it, so that he wouldn't have to guard it every moment. I designed the lock and "blunder" expertly made the pieces to my specifica-tions. While I assembled the lock, "blunder" forged the chain. In my pres-ence, he never struck the iron too hard, he forged a heavy chain for the lock. Then "blunder" was free to leave the smithy, the bonded blacksmith came almost immediately; the second time "blunder" left the smithy to go off with us, with Tamt and me, the bonded blacksmith tried several times to get into the forge, but the chain wouldn't break and my lock was too clever to pick and too strong to be broken. I had made all manner of things for my wife, for the house we shared, or had things made in my own way. I never trusted anyone to make anything properly, only an idiot trusts other people to make the things he surrounds himself with.

Shortly after Tamt and I took up with him, "blunder" made his first sword. He worked it endlessly with strokes of such force that Tamt and I were driven outside, I remember how exhausted I was from wincing. Every blow on the iron clanged on the air and Tamt and I would recoil. There was no getting near "blunder" while he was working. The sword he made was blunt and unpolished, it was the color of lead, or soot. He made it and put it aside, he paid little attention to the hilt, the hilt was actually extremely crude. To our surprise, to his surprise, I suppose, as well, the Baron's functionary purchased it right away, the Baron had lost his sword, according to the glazier, or broken it, according to the fruit seller, and urgently needed a new one, it was unclear why, or no one knew why. By that time I had acquired spies, and I could ask the spirits. The Baron had received "blunder"'s sword and been very dissatisfied with its bluntness and crudeness, the Baron had called it a "crudely made, blunt sword." There was no question that this was an accurate description. The Baron used it only in practice, because it was extraordinarily heavy. My spies told me that the Baron had noticed that, no matter what, "blunder"'s sword never chipped, never bent, and he tested it further, more and more ruthlessly, to try to break it, but it simply would not break or bend. The Baron had done everything short of melting it down, but the sword would not break or bend. The Baron had the blade sharpened, and this with great difficulty, and found that the edge would not dull, that nothing would diminish its sharpness or nick the edge. The Baron began to carry "blunder"'s sword. He brought off a number of glorious feats with "blunder"'s sword, and "blunder" was all at once receiving requests for swords. "Blunder" accepted only very few of these; he seemed to work in a trance, and without any thought of profit. The bonded blacksmith left the third marketplace. When he found his wife alone with her lover the Baron impaled her with the sword "Blunder" had made, this I heard from my spies, although it wasn't long before everyone in Lohach was telling each other again and again that the Baron had impaled his wife on that sword, and had pursued his wife's lover, as he fled, while she was yet impaled on the sword, and had also impaled him, her lover, on the same blade, so that the two of them were impaled, with a brief interval between, on the same blade side by side. The Baron had then driven the point of that sword into a stone of the castle wall, the stone walls of the Wersecastle, pinning there his wife and her lover, before he hurled himself into the Werse. The Baron drowned himself in the Werse, and his wife and her lover are still pinned to the stone wall of the Wersecastle, on the sword "blunder" forged for the Baron, so that the Wersecastle was soon abandoned, because no one could bear to hear their screams, and no one could manage to pull the sword from the stone wall of the Wersecastle. My spies tell me that the Baroness' family have sent workers to the Wersecastle and had erected scaffolding there, against the stone wall, with the intention of removing the stone in which that sword is embedded and freeing the Baroness and her lover. The Baroness' family intends to free the sword by battering apart the stone, once it is removed from the wall, but the scaffolding is needed first lest the wall collapse and crush the Baroness and her lover, who are still alive, impaled on that sword. My spies tell me that the stone in which "blunder"'s sword is embedded has begun to turn into iron. The spirits tell me that the Baroness and her lover are turning into iron, the sooty lead-colored iron of "blunder"'s sword. I had always felt that they ought to have asked "blunder" himself to extract the sword from the wall. I still can't imagine why they never did. "Blunder" was filled with Wite's spirit—when I told him about Wite, he believed at the first moment, he listened to everything I said in silence, and when I had finished he went off by himself. I came across him later that night, after sunset, when the market is closed, I found him behind the smithy in a small sheltered spot, I found him gazing at Wite's mountain, which was shining a little with snow on the horizon, the gleam from Wite's mountain was the same color as starlight and only a little dimmer than starlight, and the stars were very bright that night, I remember. The sky was clear and the stars were all visible and very bright, and from where "blunder" was standing Wite's mountain was visible in the distance, deep in the forest. When "blunder" turned to me his features were indescribably transfigured, he stared at me I especially remember how liquid and bright his eyes were, what a fierce light there was in his eyes and behind his face! "Blunder"'s unscarred face was bright and fierce, and transfigured, I'm trying to say he was somehow taken out of himself, he seemed to have *gone over*. When he recognized me, he didn't speak, but his transfigured face shone with gratitude, and all at once he did speak. It's not for me to repeat what he said; it's better, I think, they remain with me.

"Blunder" was the first convert in Lohach. With his chain and my lock he would close up his smithy and come with Tamt and with me to our water tower. We would sit together there. I was almost ready to begin building the lamp, but the idea was still only just conceived in me and I needed to work out the design with care. The only things worth doing—well I would sit on the roof gazing off at Wite's mountain, and of course at Tzdze's mansion invisible in the distance, behind ramparts of beautiful trees. I would stand on the roof and I would want to reach out my hands and lift the forest into the air and quench my face against it, raise it to my face as I would raise the hem of Tzdze's dress to quench my face against it and breathe the fresh air, the air in Lohach is lifeless, I want a great wind to blow all this stagnant, fetid air away, but the air in the forest, and the air in the mountains, is fresh. With that air in my sick lungs life would be possible again even after all this sick time. "Blunder" was the first convert in Lohach. I didn't gather my converts around me, except Tamt and "blunder". I sent out into the city like a spy and made conversions there, with Tamt's help, with "blunder"'s help. I walked through all of Lohach every day with my eyes open. I found a young woman, the first after "blunder" in Lohach, I found a young woman first. "Blunder" was the first, I've said that.

Her family were monsters, they had decided she was insane. Her family had locked her in the basement, I was drawn to her window, by the curb, next to the garden, by her musical shrieks late at night. The window was dingy, it was cracked toward the top and barred, there was a small chink removed in the crack and I was able to see into the basement through the chink, I could see her there wandering back and forth. I came back a number of times and would see her there at any time of day, sometimes giving little screams. Screaming with frustration and impotent anger, there was nothing alarming or hard to understand about that. I attracted her attention finally, she would bring her bestial face up to the window and gibber at me through the chink as best she could. I would stand and listen as long as I could, although she never spoke intelligibly. I didn't try to speak to her. I passed her a note, finally, through the chink. I passed her many notes over a number of weeks, I had no way of knowing what she did with them, or even if she could read them, but over time the face she brought to meet me at the window became more composed and she stopped babbling. She didn't speak a word to me, soon. She received my notes quietly. One day, when the air was clear, the sky was completely blue and clear, I came to her window, I was going to her window by the garden when I saw the mountain on the horizon, clearly, where I never saw it before. I called her to the window and pointed it out to her, she could crane herself to one side and see it, and when she saw it there was a little glint from halfway down the mountain, it was bright enough to throw reflections on the wall,—she saw it and made a little scream, the sound boomed out from the far distance and she made a little scream when she heard it and saw the glint, and she fell back from the window shaking. I didn't go back. I learned through my spies that her family had taken her out of the basement, that she seemed rational. She was acting rationally and her family was satisfied that she was cured. Later my spies informed me she had been taken on a family outing to the forest. They had gone together to the forest for a day and within moments she had disappeared without a trace—I can't describe my hysterics when I heard that! She'd convinced them to take her to the forest and then disappeared; I could see her grow lighter than air and blow away into the forest forever. One by one they would go haunt the forests with blank animal faces living in the trees, with Wite.

Between the fashionable places and the bad parts of town, there is the so-called half-world; this half-world business is a romantic notion, but as a business it is also an instrument of torture, that guides our eyes away. I went into it avidly looking and found only one there, at the wine bars where the students met, and these were only the worst possible people, these students, but I met a convert in the wine bars, of all the whores in Lohach, she was the most sought-after, she was supposed to have a mysterious indefinable feminine appeal. When I first saw her I didn't see any mystery. I knew she was the most sought-after because she was still ashamed. Her shame hadn't faded, her clients wanted to be part of it, she could still be disgraced, you see. I saw that the first time I saw her drawn face. She had been beaten back behind her features. I sent Tamt to her with a "love-letter" of my own, I sent Tamt because I knew they couldn't turn him away, she was never away from her clients and proprietors, but I sent Tamt to her and they all gave way in front of *his errant face*. Tamt brought her my notes and when the time came I let him show her. She and I never met, she never wrote back to me, but she received Tamt every time I sent him to her. When the time came I let him show her, and when he came back he told us—he had pointed to the mountain and she'd seen it, he'd seen the glint across all that distance and she'd seen it, when she saw it, Tamt said, she screamed. Tamt couldn't describe her scream. Tamt told us she had screamed and then started laughing, he said she smiled and showed her long teeth. Tamt said she showed her long teeth! She smiled and showed her long teeth and laughed, he imitated her laugh for us, it seemed to racket up from his gut and begin and end in his throat, he expelled it out through a wide-open mouth so that it rasped in his throat. I didn't get another opportunity to send Tamt to her. My spies told me what had happened. She had been delivered to a client in a coach, she was riding with a client in his closed coach, they were crossing the second flood bridge that night on the way to his house; she had all at once opened the door and leapt out of the coach, over the edge, down into the Werse, without a word. She had, in complete silence, and without fumbling, or any kind of haste, opened the coach door and jumped from the moving coach over the raised stone edge of the bridge, and dropped directly into the Werse. She had plunged straight into the Werse, she had plunged straight out of her dress in midair and down into the Werse. Her dress had been loosened in the coach and had slid upward off of her body as she dropped into the Werse, and it blew against a stone piling beneath the bridge and caught there, out of sight—my spies made particular note of this. The coach was stopped instantly, in the middle of the bridge, and her client and his people had looked out over the raised stone edge, down into the Werse, to the unmarked spot where she had vanished beneath the water. They watched until she surfaced again. They hadn't thought to move to the downstream side, but when she surfaced again she wasn't on the downstream side, she hadn't moved downstream, she had moved upstream, she appeared somewhat upstream, she was leaning into the current and they said her arms disappeared into the water, she pulled herself forward against the current and the water was whipped into froth around her shoulders. They said that she cut through the water like a knife, swimming upstream, they said she swam upstream like a fish, one said she swam like a dolphin, without flagging or veering to the banks she swam directly in the center of the current, which was always extremely strong there, they were able to follow her from the bridge because she was so pale, and her white slip was still clinging to her, they saw her clearly against the dark water, the current was churned to white froth around her shoulders. They said she swam past the first flood bridge out of the city and disappeared.

At this time I first was inspired to build the lamp, this was my "little task," I was instructed to build the lamp, although the lamp was of my own design, I first dreamed up the lamp of my own accord and was only then told to construct it; walking through Lohach as I was compelled to do, walking through the streets day and night as I was compelled to do, I would sometimes glimpse a little gleam in a windowpane—or shining in a polished brass door-knob—here and there I would sometimes glimpse a little gleam in a puddle, now and then a familiar little gleam. A reminder, Wite was there, Wite was present, I remember how my breath would catch in my throat, I would glimpse the little gleam in a windowpane or a polished brass door-knob and the corners of my eyes would swell as if I were on the verge of breaking out sobbing, a reminder, Wite was there, "I am *here*," I would shake and my eyes would swell, recognizing a little gleam in a windowpane. I had already conceived of my lamp, I had designed it in my so-called mind, now it occurred to me, this I don't remember in detail, it occurred to me how to build the lamp and for what purpose to build the lamp. I started working on the lamp at the water tower, with the intention of fixing the finished lamp to the top of the water tower, and this I clearly knew was an instruction from Wite, although I still cannot remember how I received this instruction, I know Wite sent word to me to build my lamp and fix it to the top of the water tower. I was told the lamp was a sign for the converts in Lohach, I wasn't instructed in detail, I was only instructed that the lamp was to be fixed on top of the water tower when it was finished and that it would be a sign for the converts of Lohach.

These converts were no *conversions*, they were no different after meeting me than they were before, if anything they were more like themselves, they were more like themselves after I spoke to them than before, they were more concentrated and less vague after I spoke to them than before. When I told them about Wite, they didn't change, they remained the same, or perhaps more so, but they did become more volatile. Wite's story volatilized them all. When they had heard Wite's story from me, and somehow knew it was true, I can't say why or how they would know it was true, but when they somehow knew it was true, they suddenly would become volatile, and leave the city or come away in some other way—Illan came with us, while others chose to leave. Illan was rich, a young man, his parents were some hideous citizens, the typical sort of provincial tapeworms who run cities like Lohach, Illan had called them "provincial tapeworms," his parents and all the so-called important people in Lohach. I remember we used to see Illan every day in the market, Illan wandering up and down in the market, alone and sometimes laughing, I remember seeing Illan laugh from time to time, sustained laughter at nothing, looking all around him, he would look all around him and laugh at nothing, and I remember his laugh struck me as the sound of a *wounded animal*. It was grotesque, and painful to see. Tamt and I took Illan to the water tower, and to the smithy, we told Illan about Wite, we took Illan in and looked after him; I wish I could remember half the things Illan said—he became our little spider, he turned into a perfect spy, Illan pretended to reconcile himself to his parents and pantomimed so-called good living with frightening ironic ferocity, he pretended to be a good son and he lived with his parents and punctiliously did everything they asked, and spied for us all the while, he would spend his days deceiving everyone and smiling to their faces, then come to us in the evening and vomit up his glad tidings, laughing all the time like a wounded animal. Illan was a little fleshy and pale with dark hair and shining eyes like a nocturnal animal, he was a resourceful mimic, I remember he had a sweet piping voice with which he would imitate for us perfectly and viciously the empty mercenary society ladies and mindless complacent clockwork citizens of his society nights. Illan spent his nights in society spying for me, he would creep through the city all night without sleeping, spying wherever he could and bringing us back little morsels of information, anecdotes to laugh at, we laughed out loud with him, he told us his anecdotes and stole for us, filled up our water tower with the things he'd stolen for Tamt and for me, and with gifts for "blunder"—a piece of iron, a bag of coal, "gifts for "blunder." What became of you, Illan? I was working on the lamp by that time, I would get the individual pieces from "blunder" and assemble them myself, and Illan would bring me the compounds I needed for the battery, he would steal them from this place and that and bring them to me, a little at a time. I worked on the lamp, which I had designed, and wandered through the city from time to time, and now and then I found someone to tell. I never told anyone about Wite who didn't need to hear. Illan was circulating throughout the city, he was our spider, our spy, it was from him I learned that Felix's unmarried sister-in-law's story was circulating in Lohach, that the Alak representatives were asking questions, bringing up my name in connection with the stranger in Felix's unmarried sister-in-law's story, I learned from Illan that I had been *presumed dead*, the Society and the Alaks had been good enough to presume I had perished in pursuit of Wite, but they were asking questions about me, and that suggested they were no longer certain, or that there were some who felt one way, that I was dead, and others who felt another way, that I was not dead. Mine was not the only body they failed to recover, though I was the only survivor, there had been no serious search for remains of the Prince's party after the first snowfall that winter, I had assumed as much. I only learned from Illan that I had been presumed dead. I learned from Illan that Tzdze had been visited by the Alaks, that she had been questioned, Tzdze questioned by the Alaks! I pressed Illan, I made demands, I pressed him to find out more, he told me that Tzdze was still at the estate, that the Alak party had only dropped by, that they had already known, from one of the servants, that Wite was dead. As he loved to do, Illan went to great lengths to find out more, he told me that the Alaks were "bruiting about" the idea that I might still be alive, and the infernal Society had declared that should I still live, I could only be a soul burner; it was easy for them, with the greatest possible ease they put my name on the list, their nauseating death list, from which list they struck Wite's name years ago. If I lived, I was necessarily a soul burner by now, by Wite's example, so they said; the Society came unavoidably to the stupidest possible conclusions, they always insist on concluding a matter before they enter into it, they first come to their utterly worthless conclusions, without so much as a word to anyone, and then they go forth and find exactly what they expected and pat themselves on the back. They blithely placed my name on their nauseating death list even though I never became a soul burner, not that I didn't deserve to die I suppose, everyone does, but naturally only after an equally nauseating discussion around the table, deciding what to do about me, that if I was not dead, as they wanted me to be, they clearly wanted me dead, they would have preferred me to be dead, but if I was still living, they would see to the correction of that mistake that regrettable oversight.

I learned from Illan that there was no serious effort to find me in Lohach. Illan and I, and Tamt, would sit on the main avenue with our peanuts soaked in coffee, and Illan would sit smothering his laughter and telling me secrets in broad daylight, we would sit and watch the Alak representative guard goose-stepping on the main avenue in the square before the adjutant's house, their boots would fall in unison after a fully-extended and slow ascent, Illan would speak to the regular rapping of their polished boots, in between the steps. We sat for hours and watched the guards goose-step for hours in front of the adjutant's house, for hours, until they were relieved by the next uniform batch.

I worked on the lamp, I assembled the battery and began working on the timer, the lamp was a spark across two rods, the rods would burn away over time, the timing mechanism would push the rods together at the same rate at which they burnt, maintaining a consistent gap, a steady light, by means of clockwork. I stayed at the water tower, the timer was complicated and hard to build, I had to work at it all the time, I lost every moment to fitting the gears of the timer together absolutely precisely. I did not leave the water tower during this time, the gravediggers would leave us simple provender on the back steps or would come up to the water tower to see us; as I said before, we had a special affinity with gravediggers, there wasn't a gravedigger in Lohach who didn't come to visit us, who didn't share some of his provender with us, who didn't put himself at our disposal. I had only to speak to one gravedigger some time before, and soon there wasn't a single gravedigger in Lohach who had not placed himself at our disposal, we could have called up an army of gravediggers—no armies, no societies, nothing of that sort. I wasn't going to permit anything of that sort. No armies, no societies. We were no army and no society. From my death-bed, writing in this narrow cell filled with sickening air, I tell you we were no society and no army, and there is to be no society and no army. I didn't want to know them—the prostitute, the woman in the cellar, Illan, "blunder", Tamt—I wanted to let them go. I didn't want to hold them. I didn't want to hold Tzdze. I didn't want to hold Wite. You'll get none of their stories from me, this is *my* story, I won't presume to speak for them, I won't profane them by presuming to speak for them, if you want to know who they were from me, I will tell you who they were for me, that's all anyone can say about anyone else or has any business saying. I wouldn't have them fall into a society around me because I won't speak for them, no one should speak for them, no one could, how can anyone speak for anyone? But the moment people congregate together in societies and cities, these half rat-warren half open-sewer cities, what do you have? Everyone speaks and no one speaks. Look, you hypocrite, how you hate cities and everyone in them, and meanwhile here come gravediggers and helpers of all kinds—fine, then, am I a hypocrite? Didn't they come to me because they felt the same hatred, and wanted the same relief I wanted?

I don't know, I was never told, if "blunder" had received instruction from Wite or had only been acting in Wite's spirit, whether he meant it as a sign or as an invitation or had meant anything by it—"blunder" went in the middle of the night to the first market square in Lohach, I had seen him going and I followed him. I had nothing better to do, I had seen the look on his face. I followed him. "blunder" went to the first market square carrying his hammer. "blunder" had his hammer with him, over his shoulder and was going in the middle of the night to the first market square. I watched him without letting on, he didn't notice me, I had no way of knowing but I don't believe he noticed me following him, I don't believe he did indulged himself with any thought for me or for us. I followed him and stood at the edge of the square, I stopped at the edge of the square when I saw him walking directly to the base of the first public cistern; this cistern was vastly larger than the water tower, it was the largest cistern in the city, it stood alone on three pilings towering over the square, I have no idea what it was for, I stopped at the edge of the square when I saw "blunder" walking directly across the square to the base of the first public cistern, to the stone foundation, each piling sank into its own stone foundation. I can't say, now, just what the cistern was for .

"blunder" took a long wedge from his belt and stabbed the piling with it, driving it a little into the wood, the pilings were made of the hardest possible wood, from practically petrified wood, "blunder" stabbed the piling with his wedge at chest level, so that the wedge was parallel to the ground, and he began driving it into the piling with his hammer, striking it with regular blows that resounded and that came steadily at even intervals driving the wedge into the piling, he stood swinging his hammer and driving the wedge into the piling at about the level of his chest, his wedge was parallel to the ground, each blow drove it visibly deeper into the nearly petrified wood, visibly deeper, even to me at the edge of the square, "blunder" standing nearly exactly opposite to me across the square, I saw him drive the wedge into the piling with regular blows, and all at once without breaking his rhythm "blunder" changed direction and began striking down on the upper surface of the exposed end of the wedge at its exposed end I think I've said, driving it down, without breaking the rhythm he started driving the wedge down until cracks tore through the piling altogether, "blunder" knocked the wedge away and struck the piling directly, sideways blows. The piling broke, and slid off its stump, "blunder" turned and ran, his feet striking the ground with regular blows, his eyes fixed, he didn't see me, he ran past me up the street, the piling slid off its stump, leaving it sticking up truncated from its stone foundation, the piling swept above the ground as the whole structure twisted, the tower yawed to one side, the two moored legs of the tower, which were still supporting the cistern were twisted. They groaned, and one snapped, with a sound like a cannon shot, the cistern veered over, the whole thing was shrieking where it had groaned before—this all happened at once, it veered over and the stone foundation of the final unbroken leg was uprooted, entire, the cistern crashed down into the buildings on the east side of the square, shattering them to their foundations sending debris flashing into space on all sides and water swept through the square, I was already running away, I could still manage to run, I stopped only to watch the water sweep through the square for a moment, the cistern shattered the buildings on the east face of the square, tore open the adjacent buildings behind them and flooded the entire square, sweeping the wreckage from the shattered buildings, and their contents, into the lower stories of the surviving buildings and flushing some of the contents of the surviving buildings out into the square; the water ebbed out into the streets almost immediately and disappeared into gutters and grates.

I lost sight of "blunder" completely. I have never been what you would call a fast runner. I have never been fast—I escaped being caught in the water but I couldn't follow "blunder". I watched him vanish in moonlit streets. I didn't know what to make of it all. I only half wanted to go after him, I watched him running away, I had no idea where he was running, I thought he might leave Lohach forever, running straight to the horizon. I remember imagining "blunder" running straight to the horizon, and on the horizon was the sun, and the sun's light was my lamp's light. I don't suppose that's important.

I followed this reasoning in inarticulate images. I saw the sun, then my lamp, and I knew in the way one simply knows things, clearly and distinctly, in dreams, that the lamp had to be ready by the next night,

I had to get it working as quickly as could be managed, and then I was off on *my* way, on *my* straight-line track, back to the water tower. I went directly back to the water tower and sat down to work on the lamp, and when its light was working I got up again, it was already nearly sundown, I had worked through the rest of the night and through the next day entirely. I had worked without looking up once and the lamp was in perfect order, and I wasn't tired. I have no special endurance, but I wasn't tired that evening. I climbed to the top of the water tower with the lamp tied to my back and I fixed it to the peak of the roof, facing Wite's mountain on the horizon. It was always looming just on the horizon, where it shouldn't have been visible, it should have been too far away and lost in haze, but it stood out clearly even as the sun was setting.

I was suddenly free, the lamp was finished and working perfectly, my time was my own again. I thought of "blunder" at once, I ran to his smithy, that is I ran to the third market, around the corner; again I say I wasn't at all tired. The vendors and the crowd had pulled back, down the avenue, away from "blunder"'s smithy, most were busy packing up their things, there was frantic activity further up the avenue where the vendors were closing early, because there had been some sort of altercation, a man had been assaulted there, in front of "blunder"'s smithy. I didn't enter the street, I slipped up to the next street, Illan our spider had found a little aperture in a wooden fence between two houses. This had been the route he'd taken, I could grasp things that way, through the aperture, behind the smithy. I came up behind to the little window by the forge and peered in, the place was a shambles, worse than usual, I mean disarray, signs of strife. "Blunder" was sitting on the ground leaning against his anvil, gazing out the open door, he was at an angle to me, I could see the look on his face as he gazed serenely out the door, up at the sky. The next moment he caught sight of me, smiling and turning his head a little in my direction, shifting the gory hammer in his hand. "Blunder" had been seen, although I've always wondered if men hadn't come for him on general principles. More would come soon, they most likely were getting themselves together at that very moment, it's something I simply knew was happening just then, that a number of men were on their way to the smithy, with violent intentions. I tried to indicate this to "blunder" through the window, although I had a strange reluctance to raise my voice above a whisper.

I gestured for "blunder" to come with me. He was gazing out at the sky again, he wasn't paying much attention to me. I stood by his window like an idiot trying to get his attention. "blunder" stood up and left, walked out into the street and out of my sight. I didn't want to leave him alone, I was afraid for him, what could I have done for him? I followed him anyway, I went round the smithy and emerged on the street.

"blunder" was at the glazier's shed, just inside. I ran across the street and around to the side of the shed, again at the window. He was standing directly on the other side, gazing up past my head, he was still, beaming up at the sky, his eyes wide open and beaming, still, looking up at the sky, smiling with perfect simplicity, beaming. In my memory it begins to seem as though we were going to go from one place to another and one window to another and repeat the same moment over and over, as if that would forestall the catastrophe. I asked "blunder" and repeated my question, about the cistern. He looked surprised at me but he didn't stop smiling or gazing. I heard sharp alterations in the air. All at once "blunder" had stepped into the street again, there were four men in front of his smithy. "blunder" walked up behind one of them, evidently unnoticed, struck him over the head with his hammer, and killed him. These men had brought with them a few leashed dogs, and these now lunged this way and that, hysterical with alarm. One of the men turned in "blunder"'s direction, flinging up his arm before his face, "blunder" swung his hammer instantly, striking the man in the stomach with a terrible sound. Another man, I recall him I think he had been peering into the smithy, and even calling for "blunder," although not by name, and who turned back to the street when he heard the commotion, that being the moment I first saw his ruddy face and drooping moustache, the sort of one I never liked, and this one held a pistol in his hand. He raised it and shot, that is, it went off as he raised it. "Blunder" stepped behind a post, one of a number of them at that part of the street, and the man he'd hit in the stomach was lying there, belching, on his face, in front of the posts. There was another man I lost track of, there were four to begin with but more may have arrived in the meantime. No reason exists why all of the men who had assembled elsewhere to confront my friend had to arrive at the same moment. Another man, in fact, did appear from the street below me, and stood not far from where I remained in the glazier's shop, looking on at the encounter with an expression of hesitation. This had all taken only a few moments, I was surprised, I was stupidly trying to think of something, I knocked one of the glazier's panes off the back of his display table and when it shattered on the ground, the man standing near to me, who had a puffed up look, turned automatically to gape at me, and "blunder" ducked around one o the posts, moving with astonishing speed, and hit the man who held the pistol, and who was still standing in the doorway of the smithy, in the ribs with his hammer, so that, from my point of view, the man with the pistol vanished instantly, driven into the smithy like a billiard ball into its pocket. The other of the four men who first came for "blunder," and about whom I can remember no particulars, simply ran away. The man standing near to me cried out in astonishment and turned, I think, to rejoin whatever others there were. He gaped a moment at me, first, not that he knew me, I'm certain he saw only a stupid-looking, frightened old man, then turned and began to run, but fell a moment later, something had tripped him I think, or perhaps he lost his balance trying to avoid tripping over something, as often happens, and "blunder" darted up to him and struck the side of his head with his hammer and killed him as well. "blunder" stood upright in front of me, I remember his hammer and hands were dotted with black blood, he was breathing hard and his eyes were like balled-up ribbons of water, I thought precisely in those words, looking at him, when my mind had settled a bit; our minds cleared—no, his did, if it needed to. My mind was clear, if startled.

We stood in the street in front of his shop and the glazier's shed without speaking. "blunder" turned his face up again just as it began to rain enormous icy drops. I went up to "blunder", who was allowing the rain to soak into his face, turning his face bright red from the terrible coldness of those drops, I pawed a little at "blunder"'s arm, a clean bit of sleeve, and then although my voiced cracked and sounded completely unnatural I spoke up, and told him we'd have to leave.

"blunder" came with me. There would be armed men at any moment, the whole city would turn out in earnest in a matter of moments. That sort of thing was taken personally, and the Alak representatives were certain to arrest or kill "blunder" if they could. This was absolutely necessary, from their point of view.

Illan had found a little crevice.

There was a little crevice, in the wall near the Werse, the city gates would certainly be locked before we got to them, but Illan had found a little crevice in the wall near the Werse, this crevice trailed down along the stone bank of the Werse, and out of Lohach—"blunder" and I knew about this crevice. I had no doubt "blunder" would be safe from those men once outside the city, I was sure he could make his escape once he managed to get out into the countryside, I knew he had to leave at once, "blunder" would have to escape on his own immediately or be killed by Lohach all together, which hadn't turned against him or us, it had always been against us, but only now was it angry enough to single us out, I shared the blame for "blunder's so-called crimes, without a doubt, that was why I didn't leave him, whether they knew it or not. I led him to the crevice and we slipped in together; this was a flaw in the stone, where it had cracked and spread apart over time; we reached the crevice, it wasn't far, by alleys and by the emptier streets. I was still wide awake, I was still not tired. "Blunder" and I made our way through the crevice, out from under the city walls down along the course of the Werse; there were no breaks in the wall, we had to go all along the length of the crevice to the end. "Blunder" and I slipped out from under the city walls, we followed the crevice along the course of the Werse, there were hoofbeats and a horse appeared coming in the opposite direction, carrying an armed man, with more behind, the crevice was too narrow for them to come more than one at a time, this one, the foremost, shot his bullet at me and knocked me over, it struck me in the thigh and broke the bone, I fell seeing stars, you can't imagine how it hits you, as if there couldn't be so much force in the world, I saw "blunder" take a sort of skipping leap up the side of a boulder protruding from the crevice-walls, he leaped with his hammer hanging low and swung it up as he leaped, the man who'd shot me was coming at him directly but "blunder" was faster, he leaped right up and brought his hammer up, it hissed through the air, you see how well I remember, it swung up inside the man's right arm and struck his chin, his helmet exhaled a pink cloud, "blunder" drove the hammer back across the head, the chin was down on the chest and "blunder's hammer struck the top of his helmet and caved it in completely. "Blunder" did something I couldn't see just then, I think he was off his balance and trying to get back, away from the next man, I seem to recall he thrust his back against the wall to keep from falling, he jumped down and there was another shot. "Blunder" was in the dark, in a shadow, and I couldn't see whether or not he'd been injured then. I became confused, but I think he'd struck the man's horse, or perhaps he'd sent the first one's horse back out into the second one, the second horse. The mounted man was struggling to get control of his horse, and "blunder" broke is leg, then pulled him to the ground and hit his head. I wanted to call to him, but I'd been shot and was weakened, I was falling over fainting, "blunder" evaded them, those two men I mean, and killed them almost all at once. I was extracting the bullet from my leg. I looked up when I had pulled it out, and I saw the crevice was clear to its end, slickening where it opened with rain, and the smell of rain was blowing in cold fresh air, the first fresh air since I'd come to Lohach, more or less, and "blunder" was standing beaming back at me. On the ground, here and there, I saw the spirits of the dead men mouching around, peering here and there with evil, idiotic faces. I devoured them right away and mended my broken leg with them, and when I looked up again "blunder" was still standing beaming back at me, his eyes like two ribbons of water balled up, gleaming, he was shifting his weight from foot to foot, holding his hammer still, the look on his face—I can't tell you, he *beamed*, his face shone with tranquility. I remembered the lamp—I told him to go on. "Blunder" turned immediately and ran out of the crevice; I never saw him again, I know he escaped.

I had repaired my leg, there was nothing wrong with me, I wasn't tired at all, I made my way back up the crevice and under the wall, there were no armed men there, although there was commotion, I don't know where they were, I came out into the street and went on without pause, I was bumbling and stumbling as I always did, I've never been graceful, I made my way back to the water tower with increasing urgency, I was walking in the rain which came in gusts, blew over me in waves, the rain was blowing over me in irregular waves, I walked on through these irregular waves of rain, with my head down watching the ground and my feet, and sinking into my soaking clothes; walking in the rain like this has always made me confused, or it tends to drive my mind in circles, I was barely aware of the streets, the people who were hiding from the rain and didn't see me too well, they didn't see me nor I them I watched my feet and kept moving thinking only of the water tower, I was determined to get back to the water tower even if it cost me my last ounce of strength—why would it cost me anything like my last ounce of strength? But I thought beleagueredly that I would return to the water tower even if it cost me all my strength, I fixed my will beleagueredly on the water tower and made my way there singlemindedly, and as I was making my way there another thought was slipped in among my thoughts, I was told without my knowing it why I had to return and what I was to do, what was going to happen—the whole city seemed to be animated by this secret anticipation, for once I had a sense of Lohach as a whole, something that would affect all of it was in my mind, so all of Lohach was clear in my mind, palpable in my mind. I nearly threw myself over onto the ground when I found our door but without stopping I climbed to the roof and the water tower and to the top of the water tower, to my lamp, I was on a ladder looking up at my lamp through a hatch in the roof, we had built this hatch in the roof and I was looking up at the lamp through the hatch, at the top of the ladder, rain was pouring in on me, I could barely see but I clearly saw that the lamp was dry, I knew it wouldn't work if its contacts were wet but they were dry in the midst of all that rain, I am telling you they were *dry*. I reached up, my hand is shaking, I reached up and my hand was shaking then as well, I touched the lever and watched the contacts move together, the connection was already made, the contacts moved together and my lamp's piercing single light shot its beams, brighter than I expected, I was nearly blasted from the top of the ladder, the light was bright as the sun, I stood look-ing at it although my eyes were smarting, I stood at the top of the ladder looking at it through the hatch with the rain falling on my face, my eyes opened wide and my mouth dropped open and I beamed at it, just as I'm doing now, this was the signal, I was thinking with joy, I had seen the glint of Wite's glasses shining from his mountain, I could see it now, through the rain, in the distance, I was sending the corresponding sign, I was filled with joy looking at my light. Did Tzdze see my light? I wondered that then, did you see it and know that it meant I was still alive, still in love, and all that? I could see from there, or I knew from there, my light was visible everywhere in Lohach, in every corner of Lohach, the gravediggers saw it and flung down their spades; Illan, surrounded by horrible high-society automata of Lohach, his eye was tapped by my beams; and in every corner of Lohach those who understood knew what was coming, every one of them, they climbed out from under their clients, they dropped their daily work, they crawled to their feet from where they had fallen and made their way out—I saw it happen from the water tower, I saw them throwing up their hands, their daily work, and spitting in faces, silently running, and without knowing why others who took up their mood, even in the gusting rain, now it was getting dark, even in the gusting rain I watched fires coming up here and there, sounds of riot, sounds of splintering shop-doors and bursting shop-windows, I watched fires come up here and there, I stood on the roof with the water tower above me, I stood in the wind on the roof and watched the fires come up, poking up like little flowers here and there, each fire came up like a little rip in my soul, in my chest, torn a little hole and smooched the little tear with firey lips, don't argue with me I'm telling you how it felt I watched the fires come up and was whipped by cold rain and wind and felt my ears fill up with the sounds of riot in the streets, only the Lohach-proper people were rioting, rioting or holing up frightened in their homes, while my people were running, I could see them to my joy I saw them here and there running over the grass, outside the walls. Little dark spots I could just see in the last few moments as night was falling and I was whipped to and fro by icy rain and cold wind, smoke and fire here and there beaten in icy rain and cold wind, riot in the streets, I hope they all got away!

I hope they all got away I turned when I saw a glint on the horizon, I saw a dark sinuousness coming from the woods, the part in the woods which was a wide opening was showing a dark sinuousness, a vast black bulk like a snake with white crests on its hulk, it hulked irregularly with little white crests crawling over its body, I saw it turning and coming, widening and throwing up a long ridge on its humped back and it roared audibly without pause continuously howling with mounting strength without taking breath, covered with flickering white crescents like fire-shadows and I am not lying, this is the truth, this is what happened, I was blown into the air, I was swept from the roof into the air on a gust of wind that drew me up above the city and carried me along over the city, over the streets where there were fires and mobs, I was blown off the roof into the air the moment I saw that dark sinuousness was a wave filling the channel of the Werse and spanning it at greater breadth, swamping the channel of the Werse, and as I was swept off the roof and watched the roof vanish away from me in the downpour I saw the Werse billow and charge its banks, the wave struck the first flood bridge and smashed it to pieces and surged greedily in all directions inside the walls and over the walls in a moment sweeping down the streets to every side, this was the sign and invitation that "blunder" had made when he struck down the cistern, he either had word from Wite or had known somehow it doesn't matter how or had somehow it doesn't matter how invoked it by knocking over the cistern, the water boiled down the streets and the wave rolled down the banks bursting the second flood bridge and the third flood bridge and the fourth flood bridge like popping stitches, Lohach was swamped in a moment and the buildings were swept aside like the flat of a hand flattening them successive waves rippling along the backside of the first hammering back the buildings and toppling the heavy walls of Lohach, the fires were all extinguished in the blink of an eye and the mobs in the streets and the frightened ones holed up in their houses were swept aside and crushed and drowned, this flood in the middle of the dry season ploughed Lohach into the earth and left only nameless pieces behind and only the ones who saw my light—which went out only at the last, the water tower floated and my light was swept along still visible in the cloudburst and still burned under the black surface of the water for a moment, a shining black halo of devastating water gleamed at me and at the same time a glint flashed at me from the horizon, and then my light went out—only the ones who saw my light escaped, only they lived, stood aside and watched. I had been blown aside, I was set down by the air on the earth again at the edge of the woods. I looked up and saw Tamt above me in the branches of a tree, still asleep.

CHAPTER TWELVE

———

Where have I gotten to now? They have come up around me on all sides to watch me die, I intend to frustrate them. I have a reserve of strength that I will never use in this world, soon the sun will rise and its beam will strike the floor by my head and confuse them long enough. I will give up my spirit when the sun strikes the floor by my head and the spirits are confused. This page is standing between me and where I am going, it will fall away, I imagine it like a white plank half in the dark, laid over that gap, as I write the last word it will fall away, and that gap will open for me, this time no escape. The words will come to the end, I'll use them that way to push me as far out as possible. From Lohach I went with Tamt from town to town; my description was circulating, the Society was hunting me now in earnest, they had made a description of me and were hunting me throughout the world, some passing meddler had given them my description, perhaps Felix's unmarried sister-in-law had given them my description, the old whore, when the word came that Lohach was flooded and destroyed, some other meddler gave the Society my description, I was linked with the destruction of Lohach which was not rebuilt, which is ruined to this day; so after that the Society was hunting me in earnest. I was wandering all over the world to avoid them. Tamt was with me until U_____, we had gone that far together, this was three years after Lohach was flooded; at U_____ I told Tamt to go on by himself, U_____ was the first city we had seen since Lohach, I knew the Society would be there, Tamt was not yet wanted, I wanted him to go on by himself, he was old enough, he would go on and I would go on myself, separately. I have not given away his name—Tamt was my brother-in-law's name—I know he is still free. I parted with him at U_____ and entered the city alone. I watched him go, until he was gone in the trees. I will see Tamt again in the trees. I went into U_____ without Tamt for his sake, Tamt will never be caught on my account, he will never be caught. Tamt is still young. I'll be dead but Tamt will go on for years, he'll come here, to Tebeste; I will see him that is Tamt will bring to Tebeste what I brought to Lohach. Tamt has taken over the work that I started. I stayed at U_____ for a few days only, I had to leave almost right away, I stayed only long enough, as long as I had to, I was old enough then, I rested to get ready to go to Tebeste. I'm sure the Society missed me in U_____ only because I lay in a dry culvert for three days there, I lay there without moving and rested, I had my provisions, I wasn't hurt or ailing, I was hiding as only I can hide. It's tiresome to go on like this, the Society was searching for me everywhere in the world, they nearly found me in U_____, I rested there a few days and left for Tebeste. Only I can The only road through the mountains to Tebeste passes through U_____, I smuggled myself past and into the mountains, I was tired but not yet sick, I couldn't do anything about my age, the Society was scouring the spirits, I had nothing to eat in that regard, they kept me weak by scouring away the spirits, left me nothing, I was already old. I couldn't prevent my age from slowing me down, although I could keep myself well for the time, but the Society was starving me and I was starting to weaken even then. The Society didn't stop me, I reached Tebeste. I am not above saying that, knowing what the Society would do to me if they found me there, I went to Tebeste anyway, on Wite's instructions. I'm tiring, the sun is shifting. Wherever I went Wite and Tzdze were in my mind, I could see the mountain on the horizon all over the world. I'm tiring. In Tebeste the Society was impossible to avoid, the Society was impossible to avoid in Tebeste in ranks around the palace and they would go into the mountains over the city to stare down at the streets, looking for me, they had heard already that I might be there, they were staring down from all but one mountain looking for me, you can imagine that didn't work, they didn't find me that way—there was one mountain there on the horizon, I spoke here and there, I don't remember what I did except that I spoke here and there, the way I did in Lohach, there was no difference, but the Society could make out my voice, it's always dead silent when I'm not trying to do anything important when I'm not trying to concentrate but just let me try to concentrate and then all of a sudden they ran to meet me everywhere—I can't go on about it, they came for me, I ran to the Imperial Guards, I did everything in my power to surrender to the Imperial Guards and not to the Society. I was fighting hard to make sure I was arrested by the Imperial Guards, not the Society. I was arrested by the Imperial Guards and brought here; I was not tried by the Society, I would not be here if I had been tried by the Society, I was tried by the Imperial Guards for treason and they sentenced me to die, here I am waiting to die; this was intentional, my going to the Guards, it meant I knew I was starved by the Society long enough, I couldn't fight off this bug in my lungs, I felt it break into me in this cell, and, when the doctors discovered it, there would be no question of an execution. These doctors said that execution was out of the question, they will dissect me after I die but they have forbidden that I be executed. I'm tiring. The sun has already risen behind the mountains, soon it will come up over the mountains, I will die when the beams strike the floor by my head where I lie I will not rise again, the spirits will be confused, the beams will shine in through the window through which, if I could stand, I would see Guards marching in the courtyard, where they're always marching, where these Alaks of ours have taken over the world, saying the message of the Alaks is love, all humanity in one happy family; they decide what they will find in the world before they see it, they choose to believe they have found what they have made, the world is shiningly agreeable to them, they have already filled up your head with imbecile ideas, their world like any world is insipid. Like any world theirs is insipid, as is yours. But I spoke here and there in Tebeste, in plain view of the palace I spoke here and there in Tebeste. I was listened to. I was heard here and there. I'm speaking here for the last time, I'm going to raise myself up one last time and speak. The sky is getting light, I will die and die and die but I am ready, I'm going stronger than I came, I will die spitting the saliva of my outrage at them, moreover coughing the bloody pieces of my testament at them, my gentle guards and the soldiers down below, the city all around and the palace out of my sight and their brainless music-box of a King, I won't die cowering I have my Wite and Tzdze Tamt and "blunder" Illan and Vyo, Xchte and uncle Heckler and tired dying imaginary Nophtha on the floor writing in his cell and seizing you at the last moment, I'm rising for the last time to seize you for one more moment, the gleam of Wite's spectacles is hovering over your shoulder! No one will be spared, whatever so-called good deeds you've done, you tepidity and every so-called evil soul in the world will be devastated all the same. Wite has already lost all resemblance to his former state, he's become something else entirely, he's as blind and relentless as a hurricane—do you imagine there's something you could say that would "change his mind"? What words would you choose to address to a hurricane? What will you say when the prisoners of the world come for you without mercy? They have been caged in human insanity irrelevance and impotence and when they come out to make your only possible apocalypse they will be elementals of insanity irrelevance and impotence, they will be inhuman and come for you without mercy, with merciless faces showing no human part—how long did you think they would stay in their cages of insanity irrelevance and impotence? Wite will bring the prisoners out. How much longer do you think they will stay in? Wite will bring the prisoners out. Wite is their standing invitation, wherever they come out they will have his help if they need it, he is there, he is here with me, I'm used up now and dying, as are you, I won't live to see it, I've lived to start it, I'll find it as I pass and recommend you to it. They only needed to know, prisoners in human insanity irrelevance and impotence, once they know there will be no stopping them any more than you may convince a hurricane, they will be elemental and not human, Wite was the first, he will blot out this city, this city will be cleared away and this tower, my prison, this cell, the bars, the guards, all indiscriminately blanked, and this testament amid the ruins will out live They will come for you without pity, you've knocked that pity out of them long ago—how should I pity you? I have no pity for you, what have you done to earn my pity? Are you entitled to my pity for the paltry fact of your so-called humanity? It's not a humanity that I recognize, there's nothing human in it! My pity is reserved only for those you've pushed out of your commonsensical way, you've pushed them right aside and now you press them up against the walls of your ruts, you're right now trying to crush the life out of them against the walls of your ruts, they are the ones who have earned my pity, they have, compressed into them, a power that must explode I am telling you it must explode and lacerate the commonsensical crowd that presses in on them, lacerate them and hack them down, turn to the walls of that rut and hack them down, clear all commonsense aside with the back of the hand and put an end once and for all to cities mobs societies armies churches, put a full stop once and for all to these pestilential mobs cities societies churches armies—and when that is done, they and I will have nothing to say to one another, we will return to our homes in the mountains, under the trees, by the rocks, and live ghostly lives in unbroken silence and solitude, and watch trees rocks grass and water reclaim the ruins. Those future ruins of your city now shall have vanished under a blank expanse of trees and grass stones hills rivers lakes oceans swamps sun and weather, and shall have been blanked out of the ghostly minds of our silent solitary successors. Once and always alone they are going on, they will go on and you will drive them on, and they will betray you to what isn't human, I was part of them once and I betrayed and betrayed, I betrayed you all and I could never betray you enough.

Printed in the United States
104110LV00003B/255/A

9 780809 572359